DAVID ALMOND

BRAND NEW BOY

ILLUSTRATED BY MARTA ALTÉS

WALKER
BOOKS

First published 2020 by Walker Books Ltd
87 Vauxhall Walk, London SE11 5HJ

This edition published 2022

2 4 6 8 10 9 7 5 3 1

Text © 2020 David Almond (UK) Ltd
Illustrations © 2020, 2022 Marta Altés

The right of David Almond and Marta Altés to be identified as author
and illustrator respectively of this work has been asserted in accordance
with the Copyright, Designs and Patents Act 1988

This book has been typeset in Adobe Jenson Pro

Printed and bound by CPI Group (UK) Ltd, Croydon CR0 4YY

British Library Cataloguing in Publication Data:
a catalogue record for this book is available from the British Library

ISBN 978-1-4063-9468-9

www.walker.co.uk

MIX
Paper from
responsible sources
FSC® C171272

Praise for *Brand New Boy*

"Almond balances suspense and reveal so delicately in this page-turning laugh-aloud book."
Irish Times

"A thought-provoking look at AI and what it means to be human."
The Bookseller

"David Almond tackles deep philosophical themes with an invisibly light touch in this funny story."
Daily Mail

"A celebration of humanity and wonder, and of what it feels like to be young." **The Times**

"One of these days, someone is going to notice that David Almond has been kidnapped by children's publishing and deman... back for ad... **Sunday Tel...**

"Intriguing, slightly creepy and ultimately rather profound. Wonderful stuff."
The Big Issue

"Almond's moving page-turner ponders nothing less than humanity and free will."
Observer

"Fans of David Almond have come to expect great things from his stories, and this is no exception, showcasing children's fiction at its best."
BookTrust

"The story of their glorious day in the woods with George is told with great tenderness and delight."
The School Librarian

"There really is no one quite like Almond writing today."
The Times

Also by David Almond

For Jane Winterbotham
D.A.

For Javi and Julen
M.A.

1

At the start we think he's just another kid like us. Of course we do. What else would we think? He turns up on a Monday morning, last week of the Easter term, in the middle of assembly. Mrs Hoolihan's taking it. We can see she's excited about something or other. She's wearing a green tweed suit and shiny high heels and her hair's all dyed and curled. She keeps looking at the door at the back of the hall, like she expects it to open.

She says all the usual stuff about how terrible bullying is.

"Don't you agree?" she asks us.

Of course we do.

"Yes, Mrs Hoolihan! Yes, Mrs Hoolihan!" What else would we say?

I'm sitting with Maxie Carr, like always. We're

doing that thing where we grunt everything like we're animals or as if we don't know what words are at all.

"E I OO I A!" we grunt.

Maxie drops his shoulders and lets his hands dangle like he's some kind of ape.

"Yes, children," she goes on. "We have to be kind to each other, especially those who don't have our own good fortune, or those who have been through trouble. Aren't I right, children?"

"Yes, Mrs Hoolihan."

"E I OO I A!"

She looks at the door again. Nothing. She blinks and frowns and grins and taps her finger in the air and looks at Mr McKenna, who starts banging away at the piano. Mrs Imani is there as well, with the little orchestra she's put together. They saw their fiddles, squeak their recorders, smack their tambourines.

Mrs Hoolihan spreads her arms wide.

"Now liberate your voices, children!" she calls. "Sing up! Sing up!"

She tilts her head towards the ceiling.

"Raise your voices to the heavens above!"

And off we go with the song we sing every Monday morning:

"*All things bright and beautiful,*
All creatures great and small,
All things wise and wonderful,
The Lord God made them all."

The little ones at the front sing high and sweet like always. Me and Maxie do that thing where we sing the words as we're breathing in, so we sound like ghosts or like we're about to croak:

"O I I A U E U. U OR O AY EM OR."

Some kids around us start to giggle. Our teacher, Mr Sage, who's sitting at the end of our row, starts to glare.

Mrs Hoolihan wafts her arms, conducting us all. Then the door at the back suddenly swings open. She jumps in surprise then spreads her arms in welcome as a woman and a boy step into the hall. Mrs Hoolihan waves at us to keep singing and waves at the little orchestra to keep playing. She waves at the woman and the boy. She indicates the PE benches like she's telling them to sit down there. They do that. She wafts her hands at them like she's asking them to sing along too. They don't do that. The woman and the boy sit there with their mouths shut. They stare out at us all. They don't move.

At last we get towards the final "*Lord God made them all.*" By now, me and Maxie are grunting like two daft dying pigs. Mr McKenna gives a couple more twirls and thumps on the piano keys. The fiddlers, recorder-players and tambourine-bangers come to a halt.

Mrs Hoolihan claps her hands and tells us that was oh so wonderful, children.

"Yes!" she calls, beaming with delight. "The Lord God did indeed make them all!"

She bends down and whispers something to the woman on the PE bench. The woman smiles sweetly, and they whisper together for a while. Then

Mrs Hoolihan shakes the hand of the boy and she brings him to the front so we can all get a good look at him and he can get a good look at us.

"This," she tells us, "is a new boy."

She beams at us. This is what she's been waiting for.

We all stare at the boy. He's very pale. He's very tidy. He's smaller than me. He's wearing navy blue trousers and a light blue shirt and black polished shoes. His pale hair is brushed close to his scalp.

"His name," says Mrs Hoolihan, "is George. Say hello to George, children."

"Hello, George," goes everybody.

"E O OR," go me and Maxie.

George says nothing. He doesn't look nervous. He doesn't smile.

"Welcome, George," says Mrs Hoolihan, "to Darwin Avenue Primary Academy."

He stares at her, then stares at us.

"We were expecting George last week," she says. She widens her eyes and beams at him. "But it seems you weren't ready, George, were you? But here you are now, a treat for us all in the last week of term."

George says nothing.

She bends down and peers at him.

"He's rather splendid, isn't he, children?"

"Yes, Miss," say some of us.

"E I," go me and Maxie.

"Excellent. Now then, children. George will only be with us for a short time, so make him welcome. Make sure he knows all the ropes and the ins and outs and the how's your fathers and the ups and downs. I know you will do that. Will you do that, children?"

"Yes, Miss!"

"E I!"

Mrs Hoolihan beams at us.

"Excellent. Make sure that his time here is something he will always remember. He will join Mr Sage's class."

Me and Maxie nudge each other. That's our class.

"Now then, our bright and beautiful children, and our wise and wonderful teachers, off to your classes you go."

2

We pass by Mrs Hoolihan's office on the way to class. She's in there with George and the woman. The woman's dressed in a cream-coloured suit. She's holding open a black leather bag and Mrs Hoolihan is peering down into it. George is just standing there, looking out into the corridor through the open door. Maxie gives him a thumbs up; George does nothing. His face is blank.

"Looks like a right bundle of laughs," says Maxie.

"Oh, Daniel!" Mrs Hoolihan calls.

I come to a halt. I go to Mrs Hoolihan's door.

"Yes, Mrs Hoolihan?" I say.

She waves me into the office. In I go.

"This lady is Miss Crystal," she says.

I say hello. Miss Crystal smiles kindly and says she is very pleased to meet me.

"And this," says Mrs Hoolihan, "is George."

"Hi," I say. I put my hand out like Mrs Hoolihan would want me to do. George looks at it.

"Shake hands with Daniel," says Miss Crystal.

George puts his hand out, and I shake it. His hand is cold. He looks me in the eye. His eyes are pale blue.

"And say hello, George," says Miss Crystal.

He says nothing.

She smiles at me and whispers something in George's ear.

"Hello," says George.

His voice is flat. He doesn't smile.

"Well done, George," says Miss Crystal.

She nods at me like she's saying well done to me, too. She writes something down on a form.

"Would you be kind enough to take George to your class?" asks Mrs Hoolihan. "Mr Sage is expecting him."

"Aye, Miss."

She raises an eyebrow.

"Yes, Miss," I say.

"Good lad. Thank you. Off you go, then."

Miss Crystal puts her hand on George's shoulder and steers him towards me.

"Thank you, Daniel," she says. "It's very kind of you."

I lead him out of the office and into the corridor.

"Is that your mam?" I ask him.

He says nothing. Neither do I.

We pass other classrooms. The kids are settling down at their tables like they do every morning. It's so weird. Why do we do this, every single morning? Troop into school, stand in assembly, listen to the same stuff, sing the same songs, sit at square desks in square rooms and get talked at by square teachers? Why does nobody see how weird it is? Why do they all act like robots? Seems like me and Maxie are the only ones that see the weirdness of it all.

"Was your last school like this one?" I say to George.

He doesn't answer. I guess it was. All schools are the same, as far as I can tell. Weird. Me and Maxie can't wait for the term to end, for freedom to come. We'll be heading off to Cogan's Wood. We'll be going wild out there. Cogan's Wood! It's just a few short streets away. You can walk to it through the lanes and alleyways between the houses. But it feels like a different world. Freedom! We can't wait.

"George," I say, just as we reach the classroom door. "You ever been to Cogan's Wood?"

He looks at me.

"Cogan's Wood," I say. "It's great. It's really wild."

"A wood is a place in which there are many trees," he says.

"True enough," I say.

"Mam is the colloquial name for mother," he says.

I stop and look back at him.

"Eh?"

"A mother is a woman to whom a child has been born."

It's weird. His mouth hardly seems to move at all.

"OK," I say.

I want to ask him a bit more, but Mr Sage flings the door open.

"Hello, George!" he says. "Welcome to your new class, lad."

3

George stands at the front with Mr Sage.

"It's an honour to have you, lad," he says to George.

George says nothing.

"Isn't it?" says Mr Sage to us all.

"Yes, Mr Sage," say some of us, though we don't know why.

Mr Sage grins. He's kind of trembling. He looks very pleased with himself today. He's wearing a green suit and a tightly knotted orange tie, and his face is very pink.

"Louise!" he calls out.

Louise looks up.

"Yes, sir?"

"I think we'll put George on your table to begin with."

"Brilliant," says Louise.

Louise sits on my table. There's a spare seat beside mine because me and Maxie were separated yesterday for cracking jokes in maths. Mr Sage points to it.

"There's a spare chair there, George," he says.

George does nothing.

"They're a nice bunch," adds Mr Sage. "Just don't take too much notice of that lad beside you." He winks at me. "He's not as daft as he likes to make out."

Mr Sage points to the chair again.

"Go on," he says. "It's yours."

George looks at where he's pointing but doesn't move. Mr Sage puts his hand on his shoulder and pushes him gently. George comes to the chair and sits on it. He looks at me like he's never seen me before. He looks at Louise and at Billy Dodds, the other kid on our table. Louise is one of the kids who play violin in assembly. Billy's wearing a badge that he made for himself pinned to his jumper. HED GARDENER.

"Hello, George," says Louise.

"Aye aye," says Billy. "What do you call a bloke with a spade in his head?"

We all groan. George says nothing.

"Doug," says Billy.

Louise rolls her eyes and keeps smiling at George. You can see she thinks he's just a bit shy. Mr Sage brings a tray of stuff and puts it down in front of George. There's a pen and a pencil and some colouring pencils, and the exercise books we use for literacy and numeracy, and also one of the big sketchbooks we use for art.

As he's doing that, Miss Crystal comes in. She sits on a chair by the door. She's got the black bag with her, and a notebook and a pen. We all look at her. George doesn't.

"Take no notice of me, children," she says. "My name is Miss Crystal, but just pretend I'm not here.

Sorry for the interruption, Mr Sage."

Mr Sage smiles at her. He lifts a pencil from the tray.

"Do you know how to use one of these things, lad?" he says to George.

George takes it and looks at it. He opens an exercise book, and starts writing straight away. His writing's neat and tidy and goes in dead straight perfect lines across the page. I look over his shoulder.

My name is George. I am eleven years old.

I am a kind and happy boy.

I am very pleased to be here.

Then he puts the pencil down.

"That," says Mr Sage, "is absolutely tip-top, George. A very good start to your time in our class."

He gives a thumbs up to Miss Crystal. She shakes her head quickly like she's telling him to take no notice of her either.

Louise leans right over the table to see George's book.

"You're a beautiful writer, George," she says, acting like she's another teacher as she sometimes does. "Isn't he a beautiful writer, Billy?"

Billy looks at his own book, at the mess and scrawl in there.

"Aye," he says. "What do you call a bloke without a spade in his head?"

"Stop it, Billy," says Louise. "Isn't he a beautiful writer, Daniel?"

I open my own book and look at the drawing I've done of the estate and Cogan's Wood.

"Aye," I say.

"Well done, George!" says Louise.

George says nothing.

I look across at Maxie. There's a flock of pigeons belting past the window. Birds. Free as birds. That's what me and Maxie want to be.

"Now then," says Mr Sage. "Let's start the day the way we mean to go on. Let's charge those brains and get them to stretch and spin and skip and sprint!"

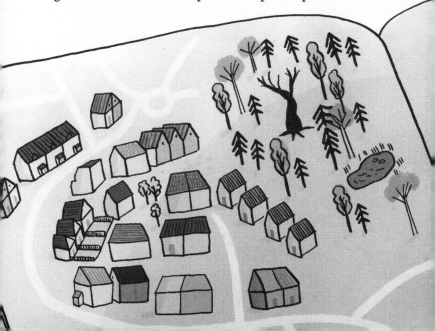

"Oh, hell," groans Billy.

Louise sits up straight and clenches her fists.

Mr Sage claps his hands, widens his eyes, pauses, then, "Three, two, one!" he suddenly says. "And off we go! 7 plus 6?"

"13!" yells everybody.

"12 x 3?"

"36!"

"7 + 4 + 3 – 9?"

"5!" calls out Louise and a few others straight after.

Mr Sage pauses again. He holds a finger in the air, then very fast he says: "10 + 10 + 7 + 10 + 9 – 2?"

"44!" Louise again.

"12 ÷ 4 x 10 x 10 – 9?"

"291!" yells Catherine Foster from Maxie's table. Mr Sage grins.

"10 + 10 + 10 + 10 + 9 – 10?"

"39!" Lots of us.

"25 x 6 x 10?"

"1500!" Louise.

"Yes!" says Mr Sage. "50 x 50 – 100?"

A pause.

"2400?" Catherine Foster.

"Correct! 9 x 7 x 3 x 10?"

A long pause. Silence, then…

"1890." George.

"12 – 3 x 8 + 100 ÷ 8?"

"21.5." George.

We all look at him.

"23 x 726?" says Mr Sage.

"16,698." George.

His eyes don't flicker. His mouth hardly moves at all. He looks at nobody. Miss Crystal writes.

Mr Sage grins, claps his hands.

"99 x 5 x 42 ÷ 6 x 10?"

"34,650," says George.

"Is that correct, sir?" says Louise.

"I have no idea, Louise."

Mr Sage writes something down. He taps on his calculator.

"74 x 45 ÷ 6 + 2356 ÷ 8?"

"363.875," says George immediately.

Mr Sage taps at the calculator. He grins at George, at all of us.

"Correct," he says. "Well done, George."

Everybody stares at George. Miss Crystal writes. George stares out of the window. The birds are belting past again.

"How on earth do you do that, George?" says Louise.

"I am a very clever boy," says George.

"Of course you are!" says Mr Sage. "Of course he is, as you all are in your different ways!"

The birds are swirling and screeching over the school roof. There's a bit of rain tapping on the window now. George stares out at the rain. Maybe he's one of those kids who seem dead slow but who have amazing talents. I lean closer to him and look closely at him.

"Where you from, George?" I ask.

He looks back at me with his pale eyes but he doesn't say anything. I ask him again but Mr Sage stops me.

"Now then," he says. "Let's not be pestering the new lad with lots of questions, eh?"

I look at my drawing of Cogan's Wood again. It's out there, just beyond the pale houses and square gardens and the straight streets, and I yearn to be there.

"And now that your minds are charged up," says Mr Sage, "let's have some history, and geography, and learn about the time of Great Adventure!"

4

Mr Sage unrolls a big square map of the world and lets it unfurl in front of him.

"As you will remember," he says, "we were following the routes of the explorers. Men like…"

"Vasco da Gama!" somebody calls.

"Columbus!"

"Maximilian Carr!" yells Maxie Carr.

Everyone laughs.

"Magellan!"

"Vespucci!"

Me, I think.

"Yes," says Mr Sage. "All of them." He grins at Maxie. "Well, maybe not quite all!"

He traces routes across the massive square map.

"Off they went to expand their horizons! Over the mountains, through the ice floes, across the oceans, into the Great Unknown! And many of the

adventurers aboard the ships were terrified. Would they ever find their way back home again? Would they be eaten by cannibals? Gobbled up by great sea monsters? Would they sail right off the edge of the world?"

"So why the hell did they go?" Billy calls out.

"Because they also dreamed of finding great treasures," says Mr Sage. "And they were brave and reckless and free—"

"And daft," says Billy.

"And mebbe," says Maxie, "they just hated where they were."

"Indeed!" says Mr Sage. "Perhaps there was that, too. Perhaps they were glad to leave behind their day-to-day lives full of troubles and cares. Perhaps some were leaving a life of crime, or times of grief or loss…"

He points to the great blue gulfs of ocean.

"Imagine it," he says. "You're aboard a tiny timber ship on a vast blue stormy sea. Imagine the terrors of the waters beneath and the gulfs of space above. The fear of death is ever present. Who among us would be bold enough to set out on something like that?"

"Not me," says Billy.

I groan. I see where this is heading. He's going to get us to imagine being on one of those ships and get us writing about it.

I don't want to set out on a ship. I just want to put my rucksack on my back and walk away with Maxie.

I see George turning his eyes towards my open book.

"That's where I want to go," I tell him.

He reaches down to touch the page.

"You like it?" I ask.

He says nothing.

"It's like another world," I say.
Miss Crystal's watching us.
She's writing something down.

I want to ask her why
she's spying on him and
me like that. I want to get in
between her and him so she
can't see what George is up to.

I point at the streams and the
pathways and the trees in my
picture. I show him the route to
the woods between the houses.

"There's Witch Tree Clearing," I say. "There's
the giant's grave. There's the lily ponds."

His eyes don't change.

"You'd love it," I say. "You really would."

5

At break time it's raining, but not hard enough to make it Wet Break. Some of us moan, but Mr Sage just laughs.

"You want Wet Break?" he says. "Do you think Ferdinand Magellan and his mates ever wanted Wet Break?"

"They should have," says Billy. "They'd have been a lot safer."

Mr Sage laughs again.

"You lot need the fresh air," he says. "You need to run about and get those legs moving and those hearts pumping."

"What about him?" says Billy.

George is still sitting at our table not looking at anybody.

"Ah, it seems that George has a delicate chest," says Mr Sage.

Billy rolls his eyes.

"Looks fit enough to me."

Miss Crystal nods.

"Mr Sage is right," she says. "We must take great care of George's chest."

"And his delicate skin," says Mr Sage. "Is that correct?"

"Indeed," she says. "Maybe when it's a little sunnier, he could go out and join the others."

"I'm sure he'd love that," says Mr Sage. "Would you, George?"

George doesn't answer.

"Go on," says Mr Sage. "Out you all go."

Out we go. Weird, how we all troop out when we're told to troop out; how we'll all troop back in when we're told to troop back in.

Out in the yard, Billy heads for his gardener's shed in the little fenced-off garden. He loves it in there. Loves messing about with his seeds and his seedlings.

I look in through the classroom window.

I see Mrs Hoolihan enter. She and Mr Sage and Miss Crystal sit at the table with George. Miss Crystal reaches out and strokes George's cheek. Then Mr Sage and Mrs Hoolihan do the same.

George doesn't budge. Mrs Hoolihan leans really close and looks direct into George's face. George doesn't move. The grown-ups talk together very seriously. Miss Crystal writes. Then the science teacher, Molecular Marx, comes in, and starts taking photographs of George. He holds George's wrist like he's taking his pulse. He seems to take a particular interest in George's ear.

Then Maxie's at my side.

He stands next to me looking into the class for a while.

"Where's he come from?" he wonders.

"Mebbe he's been in care or something. Or ill or something."

"Or he's got some condition."

We look at George through the window. We look at them all, fussing around him.

"What they poking and prodding him for?" says Maxie.

"Leave him alone!" I say, though I know they can't hear me.

"He's definitely weird, though, eh?"

"Weirder than us?"

"Eh?"

"We're the weird ones, aren't we?" I say. "Coming

into this place like zombies every morning."

"Aye," says Maxie. "*That* is definitely weird."

We look at the kids in the yard.

"If they stopped to think for a minute," I say, "they'd *all* get thinking how weird it all is."

"You're all weird!" Maxie yells.

"You're crackers!" I yell. **"Wake up! You're all asleep!"**

Nobody takes any notice.

A kid gallops past slapping his bum like he's riding a horse. He raises his head and neighs and gallops on.

Maxie snorts, then lurches in a circle. He drags his feet, rolls his head, and grunts and groans.

"Me am zombie," he groans. **"Me am living dead. Me need human flesh and blood."**

We both lurch about together for a bit.

"Me am Frankenstein," I grunt. **"Me must kill."**

Some of the lasses from Reception are doing their fairy thing, wafting their arms and dancing and catching raindrops on their tongues and squeaking like little birds.

Maxie and me limp towards them, snarling and groaning.

"Fairies!" grunts Maxie. **"Yum yum yum!"**

"Food!" I groan. "Yum yum!"

Lucinda Blair and Hellie Hall run away screaming to Nintendo Norah, one of the yard wardens, who's standing by the gates. She blows her whistle and points at us.

"You two!" she screams.

"Who two?" shouts Maxie.

"You two!"

"Us two?" I shout back.

"Aye! Leave the little bairns alone!" she screams.

"What?" I yell.

"**What, *Miss*,**" she yells.

"**What miss?**" I yell back.

"**Stop scaring them!**"

"Yes!" squeaks Lucinda. "Stop scaring us, ya big daft monsters!"

She starts giggling so Nintendo gets cross at her and Hellie, which just makes them squeak and giggle harder and cling on to each other.

Nintendo stamps her feet and waves them away.

She blasts her whistle at two lads who're

wrestling in a puddle. It's Jake Pollock and Bruce Pym. They've been mortal enemies ever since Year 2. Nobody knows why. Probably they don't even know themselves. Probably they just like wrestling now and again and getting filthy and wet together in puddles. They get up, but as soon as Nintendo looks away they laugh and snarl, and start on each other again.

Lucinda and Hellie dance back to us.

"Scare us again!" they say.

"Go on!" they say.

"Please!"

So we start the zombie walk again, and we snarl and grunt, and they shriek and scream like they're in mortal danger. When they've run off, we lurch at each other. Maxie gets dead close like he's biting my neck. I howl and groan and beg for mercy.

Then I say, "How's the new woman?"

He groans. The new woman, his dad's new partner. She's been living with them a couple of months now.

"Same as ever," says Maxie. "Oh, Maximilian," he goes, imitating her. "Do wipe your feet before you come in. And do wash your hands before dinner."

Then Lucinda and Hellie are wafting around us

again and catching rain on their tongues. They flap their hands and squeak.

"We aren't scared of the silly old zombies!" they sing.

"AAAARGH!" goes Maxie.

"AAAAARRRGGHHHH!" go I.

"Aaaaaaaaaah!" go the lasses, rushing back to Nintendo Norah.

Peeep! goes her whistle.

Stamp go her feet.

"You will all be the death of me!" she screams.

Peep-peep! Peep-peep!

The horse kid gallops past again, slapping his bum.

"Neiiigh!" he goes.

George stares out of the classroom window and we stare back. I wave at him. He doesn't wave back.

"Weird," says Maxie.

"Aye," say I.

6

Back in the classroom, it's just as I thought.

"Now," says Mr Sage, "I want you to imagine that you're living hundreds of years ago, that you're about to take part in a perilous expedition. You're going on a ship. You're leaving your family and friends behind. You are bold and brave, and you are absolutely terrified and—"

"But what if we don't *want* to go?" says Billy Dodds.

"Ah, you have put your finger right onto a crucial problem, Billy. Well done! For the truth is, many of the men did not want to go at all. But they were press-ganged, they were ambushed, they were knocked out or filled with drink, and the first thing they knew about it was when they came round and they were already beyond sight of land. Maybe *that* is what you could imagine, Billy! You have been press-ganged. You have been carried away. You awake in terror…"

Billy shivers. He curls his lip and stares across the table at me. I shrug.

"No escape, mate," I say.

Louise looks across the table too.

"Do you understand, George?" she says to George.

He says nothing.

"We have to write a story," she tells him. "Have you ever been to sea?"

"The sea is a great expanse of water," he answers. "It covers much of the Earth's surface."

Louise blinks.

"That's correct," she says.

I want to tell her to leave him alone. He isn't stupid, I want to say, but Louise has already got her hand up.

"Shall I help George get started?" she asks Mr Sage.

Mr Sage looks at Miss Crystal. She nods her head.

"Yes," says Mr Sage. "That would be *very* kind, Louise."

So here's Louise coming round the table and here's me swapping seats with her and sitting next to Billy.

"Been press-ganged?" says Billy.

"Aye."

He starts to write. I read his scrawl over his shoulder.

WALLOP! he writes. Down I went. And I knew nowt more.

Mr Sage and Miss Crystal keep looking across at George and Louise. Miss Crystal keeps writing stuff down.

George writes. His hand moves in strong straight lines across his paper. Louise whispers that that's good, George. That's wonderful, George. Very well done, George. You're an excellent speller, George. How neat you are, how tidy.

Poor George. Why can't they all just leave him alone?

I write nothing. I dream about the end of term and freedom; then suddenly Mr Sage is at my side.

"Still thinking, Daniel?" he says.

"Aye, sir. That's right, Mr Sage. Got some great ideas, sir."

"Excellent."

I pretend to start writing but Mr Sage is more interested in George. He shuffles around the table to him. George's hand is still whizzing across the page.

"Goodness gracious, George!" says Mr Sage. "Look how much you've written. What splendid work!"

George looks up at him.

"Maybe you'd like to read some of it to us, when we get to sharing time."

George says nothing.

"Maybe Louise could help you there," says Mr Sage.

Louise nods.

"He has done excellent work, sir," she says, but I have to say she looks a bit uncertain.

Miss Crystal is at the table now. She lifts George's book, reads and nods, and writes in her notebook.

"Excellent," she says. "Excellent, George."

I look down at Billy's book.

I did not wake up.

I was ded so I cud not have the advencher.

The end.

7

So we get to the bit where kids read out what they've written. There's lots of stuff about storms and crashing seas and terror. Everyone claps Sanura Gupta for her beautiful language about the pain of leaving her loved ones behind. Dickie Flynn gets his usual laughs when he manages to put farting in there, and we all wait for the bit where somebody – this time it's Vasco da Gama himself – explodes when they fart too close to the fire. Maxie writes a great bit about wrestling with a massive green sea snake that he strangles then chops its head off, and there's blood and gore everywhere.

Then Mr Sage goes, "George! Maybe you would like a turn."

George looks down at his beautiful neat pages.

"Or maybe you would like to read for George, Louise," says Mr Sage.

She doesn't seem too keen.

"Go on," says Mr Sage. "Help the new lad out."

Louise stands up.

"*The ocean is a great stretch of water between continents,*" she reads. "*Several oceans exist in the world, including the Atlantic, the Pacific and the Indian. An explorer is one who sets out for an unknown destination. A ship is a craft that can move across the sea. At the time of the great explorations, such boats were made of timber. Explorers included Amerigo Vespucci, Frederick the Explorer—*"

"Vasco da Farter!" adds Dickie Flynn.

"Dickie!" says Mr Sage. "Apologize now to Louise and to George."

"Sorry, Louise and George," says Dickie.

"Thank you. Continue, Louise."

"*The countries that were uncovered by such explorers include…*"

Barbara Sanchez puts her hand up.

"Sir!" she says.

"Yes, Barbara."

"I thought we were supposed to be using our imaginations, sir."

Mr Sage purses his lips. Miss Crystal scribbles fast.

"Well…" says Mr Sage.

"And you've said that everybody has an imagination," says Barbara.

"Yes…"

Then George begins to speak.

"The imagination," he says, and his lips hardly seem to be moving at all, "is the human ability to see what is unseen and to contemplate what is unknown. The imagination is said to be the highest human faculty."

We all watch and listen. He stares into space.

"The imagination has led to humanity's great achievements. The imagination lies at the heart of all art and all science. The imagination can be used for good or for ill. It brings into the world many joys and many dangers. The word itself comes from the Old French *imaginacion* or from the Latin *imaginatio*…"

He stops. Something flops onto the table beside Louise.

She screams.

"George's ear's fallen off!" she yells.

8

Suddenly Miss Crystal is beside George, holding his ear to his head.

Louise goggles and gasps.

"It fell off," she says.

Miss Crystal smiles.

"No," she says. "It did not, dear."

"I saw it!" says Louise.

"No, Louise. You didn't."

She does her sweet smile again.

"George *did* have a problem with his ear this morning." Miss Crystal points to George's ear, in its proper place at the side of his head. She laughs. "But how could an ear fall off?"

Louise looks across at me.

"Did you see it, Daniel?"

I stare back at her. *Did* I? I don't know what to say.

"Anybody?" says Louise.

"I saw *something*," I say. "But…"

"Billy?" says Louise.

"I was asleep," mutters Billy.

"I'm sure Miss Crystal is right," says Mr Sage. "After all, how could anybody's ear just fall *off?*" He shakes his head and grins at the very notion of it.

Miss Crystal beams at us all.

"Let's move on, shall we, children? We don't want to embarrass George any further, do we? Not on his very first day."

"Louise," says Mr Sage. "Would you like to read on?"

Louise just looks at him. She puts George's book down. *I saw it!* she mouths across at me.

"Does someone else want a turn?" says Mr Sage.

"Aye," says Patrick McAtominey.

He stands up and takes a deep breath. He raises his book, holds it in one hand, rests the other hand on his hip.

"*The storm stopped.*" He reads slowly and in a deep voice, like he always does for his doom-filled tales. "*Everything went very still and very silent. We held our breath. We knew that Death was near by. The ship began to rock. Yes, we could feel the monster, rising from below…*"

9

Outside, the rain stops. Inside, after the ear incident, things settle down. It's like nothing has happened at all. George just sits there while we finish the reading-aloud bit. He doesn't seem to be listening. When everybody who wants to read has read, Mr Sage tells us to keep on writing or to draw some illustrations to go with our work. George picks up his pencil again and belts on with his perfect-looking writing. Miss Crystal sits down beside him. She writes carefully in her notebook.

Poor George. I reckon he needs a bit of time with lads like me and Maxie.

Towards the end of the lesson, in comes Mrs Hoolihan, full of smiles.

"So," she says to us, "how are we all getting along, children?"

She beams at George.

"I hope everybody has been kind and helpful, George?" George says nothing.

"Louise Mitton said his ear fell off, Miss," says Dickie.

Mrs Hoolihan flinches and then laughs. She looks at Miss Crystal. Miss Crystal shakes her head and shrugs.

"Oh, you children!" says Mrs Hoolihan. "You and your wild imaginations!"

She talks in whispers with Mr Sage and Miss Crystal. She nods her head seriously.

"Yes," she murmurs. "Yes, I see."

I think we should get George out into the yard at lunchtime, so he can have a bit of fun and we can find out a bit more about him.

I put my hand up.

"Yes?" says Mr Sage.

"Can George play football, sir?"

"Well, I'm not really sure if he can, Daniel."

He looks at Miss Crystal.

"It's *possible*, I suppose," she says.

She looks at me.

"Would you *like* him to?" she says.

"Aye," I say.

She writes again.

"Then we'll have to see what can be done," she says.

"So can he come and join in at dinnertime?" I say.

"Ah," says Miss Crystal in her sweet voice. "But it will not be possible today."

"Why not?" says Maxie.

Mrs Hoolihan takes over.

"It's always difficult, isn't it," she says, "starting out on a new venture, settling into new places." She looks at Miss Crystal, who nods. "I'm afraid George is going to have to leave us this lunchtime."

"But he's just arrived!" exclaims Billy.

"Don't worry, children," says Miss Crystal. "George will be back tomorrow, all being well."

"When he's got his lug fixed," mutters Billy.

"He just needs a little rest," says Mr Sage. "He's a delicate soul. We have to allow him to fit in gradually."

"He'll be back tomorrow," says Mrs Hoolihan. "Full of beans. Won't you, George?"

George says nothing.

The bell goes.

"Go on, lovely children," says Mrs Hoolihan. "Out you go into the fine fresh air. Oh look, just in

53

time! The sun has decided to shine on us!"

Outside the classroom, the corridor is filled with the smells of dinner. The little ones are already in the hall for first sitting. The fairy lasses see me and Maxie and put their hands over their eyes like they're terrified. We both snarl and they goggle and scream. We head out into the yard.

Somebody's got a football and a bunch of us have started kicking it about, when a shiny black van pulls up at the school gates. A bloke gets out of the driver's seat and slides open the side door. George and Miss Crystal and Mrs Hoolihan come out of the school and cross the yard towards the van.

"George! Where you going, George?" some kids shout out.

"Had enough already, George?"

"Have you had a nice morning, George?"

"Will you come back again, George?"

He takes no notice. He just keeps walking. Miss Crystal has her hand on his elbow, guiding him forward. She gives everybody her sweet smile.

"Don't worry, children!" Mrs Hoolihan calls. "George will be back with us tomorrow!"

"Bye-bye, George!"

"Ta-ra, George!"

Some of the kids come over and gather around him. They always do that when there's a new kid. Mrs Hoolihan tries to wave them away. She laughs.

"Give the poor lad some breathing space!" she says.

Then George collapses.

He goes straight down like he's been hit by a rock or something. He crashes down onto the tarmac and lies there. Miss Crystal drops to his side and holds his head.

The bloke from the van walks into the yard. He's tall and slim and wearing jeans and a blue checked shirt. He gives us a wave like he knows us all, and like this is nothing to worry about. He gets George's legs; Miss Crystal gets his shoulders. They lift him off the ground and carry him to the van. They slide him into the back and get in with him. They shut the door.

We all edge towards the gates. Mrs Hoolihan tries to usher us back but we can see she's as scared as we are. We all stand there. Nobody knows what to do, what to say. The Reception class fairies are at my side. Hellie Hall tugs at my arm.

"Is George all right?" she says.

"Aye," I say. "Course he is. Aye."

I don't know why I say that. I haven't got a clue if he's all right or not. I try to see what's happening in the van but the windows are darkened glass. The van's engine is still running. Now lots of the other teachers are here too.

Then the van door slides open again. The bloke steps out. He gives us that wave again, then he stands aside, and here comes Miss Crystal. She smiles and reaches back into the van, and here comes George, following her.

"Sorry to worry you all," she says. "A little mishap, that's all."

She smooths George's hair.

"See?" says a wobbly Mrs Hoolihan. "Nothing at all to worry about, children."

None of us speak for a moment. Somebody is sobbing.

"George!" calls Hellie Hall. "Are you all right, George?"

Miss Crystal whispers into his ear.

He takes a step towards us.

"I am fine," he says. "I have fallen. I have risen again."

Then he stands dead still, staring at us but like he's not seeing us.

"Good boy!" squeaks Mrs Hoolihan suddenly. "It's been a difficult day, hasn't it, George? So many new faces, so many new experiences."

He doesn't answer.

Miss Crystal puts her arm around George.

"George is fine, children," she tells us. "As you can all see. But now it's time to get him home where he belongs."

She guides him back towards the van. The bloke helps them into the back. He closes the door. He gets into the driver's seat.

"Until tomorrow!" he calls.

Then he waves, and closes his own door.

We all just stand there.

"Come along now, children!" says Mrs Hoolihan. "It must be time for second sitting. In you go. Must keep those young bodies charged up."

Nobody moves. Nobody knows what to say or what to do. Mrs Hoolihan giggles.

"Off you go, children! Panic over!"

We start to back away. The van moves off. We can just see the shadowy shape of George's face, looking back at us.

10

That afternoon, we get Molecular Marx for science. I like him, especially when he comes in bonkers like he does today. He's wearing a big yellow hat and a big yellow jumper. He sits at the desk taking the register like there's nothing weird about him at all. He goes through all the names and we all say present.

"Why you wearing a yellow hat, sir?" says Dashy Wicks.

Molecular ignores him.

"We need space!" he suddenly declares.

He jumps up from his desk and spreads his arms wide.

"Space!" he says. "The great dark emptiness that surrounds us all!"

He starts shoving one of the tables towards the wall.

"Come along!" he says. "How can we orbit and dance with all this clutter in the way? Move your tables back and free some space."

We do that. We push all the tables and chairs to the edges of the classroom. Now there's a small clear space in the middle.

"We need more!" he says. "Stack those silly square tables on top of each other!"

So we pile up all the tables in one corner.

"Better!" he says.

Then he frowns.

"But, oh, to do it properly we need to shove the walls themselves away. We need to push everything to the limits of the solar system! And how, children, can we do that?"

"We can't, sir," says Louise.

"Of course we can't," Molecular agrees. "So we must make do with this silly little square space that is ours."

He sighs.

"Look how small it is. Look how narrow it is."

We all look around.

It is small. It is square. It is narrow.

"It's weird," I say.

"Weird?" says Molecular.

"Why do we go into square narrow classrooms every day?" I say. "Why do we troop in and troop out the same way every day?"

He punches the air.

"Excellent question, Daniel! I often wonder that myself. Why do you do that? Why do *I* do that?"

He ponders and scratches his chin and his head.

"Yes, indeed, it *is* weird," he says. "But we cannot pursue such profound questions today. For today, our task is to turn this little space into … nothing less than the solar system itself!"

He stands tall at the centre of the room. He holds his big yellow hat in his hands then spreads his arms wide.

"I am," he says, "the Sun!"

Kids laugh. Billy groans. Molecular points at him.

"You, Billy, will be Saturn."

Billy groans again.

"Or would you rather be Uranus?" says Molecular.

We all laugh.

He turns eight of us into planets. I am Mars. He puts the planets into order and asks us to move around him as if we're in orbit. We do that and we giggle as we bump into each other.

"Now," he says softly. "We are repeating the creation of the solar system itself. Be silent, as silent as the great gulfs and chasms of space are. Imagine yourselves turning, spinning, proceeding through the great silent chasms of emptiness that surround us all."

I do that. I glide away from the others and close my eyes. I am Mars, shining in the heavens, far away from square school and its square classrooms.

Molecular turns the other children into asteroids, comets, meteors. They move and dance between us. Molecular starts to sing, standing there at the centre of us all. No words, just weird sweet notes that flow into each other.

"Join in with me," he says. "Make your own soft beautiful music."

Lots of us giggle. I hear Maxie groaning notes like he does in assembly, but some of us try. I try. I let notes come out from my mouth and join with the others.

Soon, Molecular laughs with delight.

"Sing it!" he says. "Hear it! Well done, children. Together we are making the music that the ancients heard. We make the mythical music of the spheres, the music that was said to move the planets, the music that was said to move us all!"

And for a few moments it's really beautiful, really exciting.

It's like I'm not me, but I'm Mars, making Mars music, and dancing like Mars, and it's truly weird, not weird like the stupid weirdness of school, but weird like the weirdness of everything that exists.

Then Molecular stops singing.

He calls us to attention and we're silent.

"But Life!" he whispers, leaning towards us, gazing at each of us in turn. "Where, in all of this wonderful solar system, is Life?"

"Here," says little Izzy Mbappe.

"Yes!" says Molecular Marx. "For you are Earth. And you, Izzy Mbappe, are at the perfect distance from the Sun. You are not too hot; you are not too cold. You are drenched in liquid water. You are in the perfect place, Izzy. You are the planet that is able to teem with boundless Life."

"What about me," I say. "Is there Life on me?"

Molecular gazes at me.

"Perhaps there is," he says. "For we do think that once there was water on Mars. There may be water still, beneath the planet's surface. Maybe once a form of Life existed there. Maybe weird tiny life forms still exist there."

"Aliens?" says someone.

"Depends what we mean by aliens," says Molecular. "Depends what we mean by the word Life itself."

He takes off his yellow hat. He takes off his yellow jumper.

"I am no longer the Sun," he says. "I am Mr

James Marx, sometimes known as Molecular."

We smile. He smiles back.

"And you," he says. "Become yourselves again. You are no longer planets. You are human beings in Darwin Avenue Primary Academy in the city named Newcastle on the planet named Earth on a Monday afternoon in the century named the twenty-first."

We relax. We become ourselves again.

"And now," he says, "turn your eyes to the window and look into the sky. Imagine the universe beyond us, beyond the solar system. It is unimaginably vast."

We stare from the weird square classroom into the great weird emptiness beyond.

"It is said," he explains, "that there are as many solar systems in the universe as there are grains of sand on all the beaches of the world."

Billy groans.

"It is enough to make us all groan, Billy," says Molecular. "It is unthinkable, unimaginable. And as we look outward, we must ask ourselves: are we alone? Are there other creatures like ourselves, somewhere out there?"

"Do you think there are, sir?" says Izzy.

"Me? I think there must be, Izzy."

"Do you think they might come to us?" she says.

"Who knows? Maybe they have already come. Maybe they are among us now."

"Ah, you've found me out!" says Maxie.

He starts walking like a zombie, like in the school yard.

"Me am the alien!" he says. "Take me to your leader!"

"Aha!" says Molecular. "And where are you from, dear alien?"

"From the far-off Planet Zog!" says Maxie. He rolls his eyes. "Do not worry. I am not dangerous. Feed me cheese and onion crisps and all will be fine!"

We all laugh at Maxie, but we're all thinking, too. What if there are such things as aliens? What if they did come to us? What if, one day, we find a way to go to them?

"If there are aliens," I say, "do you think they'll be like us?"

"Who can tell?" says Molecular. "No one can know. Even now, scientists are searching the universe with huge telescopes, seeking planets that are like ours, planets on which there may be creatures that are like us. And they are looking for signals from impossibly distant civilizations."

He pauses. He allows a few moments of silence and we try to imagine the scientists, the telescopes, the impossibly distant creatures that might be like us.

"What we do know," he continues, "is that even here on Earth, Life can exist in many strange forms, that Life itself is deeply mysterious, that—"

At that moment, the classroom door opens. The school secretary, Maureen Miller, steps in.

She flinches, goggles for a moment at the state of the classroom, then she says, "Sorry to disturb you, Mr Marx, but Mrs Hoolihan would like to see Daniel for a moment."

11

I don't want to go. I want to stay in the weird classroom and think about space and weird planets and weird life and weird aliens, but of course I follow the weird secretary through the weird corridors past the weird square classrooms with the weird kids sitting weirdly at weird square tables and then I get to weird Mrs Hoolihan's weird office and she's in there with the weird bloke from the van. He's still in his tight jeans and checked blue shirt and pointy brown shoes and he's leaning back in a chair with his long legs stuck out and his hands clasped behind his head and he's smiling at me like he thinks he's not weird at all.

"Good afternoon, Daniel," says Mrs Hoolihan.

"Good afternoon," I say.

"Good afternoon, Daniel," says the bloke.

"Good afternoon," I say.

"This is Mr Eden Marsh," says Mrs Hoolihan.

"Good afternoon, Mr Eden Marsh," I say.

He grins. He unclasps his hands and leans forward. His eyes are bright blue. His hair is shiny and slick. I can smell aftershave on him.

"I've heard a lot about you, Daniel," he says.

"Have you?" I want to say. "Like what?" But I don't.

"Yes, indeed," says Eden Marsh. "And nothing but good things."

Mrs Hoolihan grins at me. She looks as excited as she was in assembly this morning.

"Good things mixed in with those laddish things, of course," says Eden Marsh. "A few little laddish mischievous things."

He winks at me.

"I was just the same meself," he says. "I *am* just the same meself."

He tilts his head.

"Nobody's perfect, eh, Daniel?"

He leans closer. He points at me.

"*Nobody*. And who would want to be?"

"Not me," I say.

"Exactly! Not you. And so it seems that *you*, my lad, are just what we are looking for."

"Me?"

"Yes. An imperfect lad. An ordinary lad. A *normal* lad. And you, Daniel, appear to be the lad that fits the bill."

I look at the head teacher. "What the hell's he on about?" I want to say.

Mrs Hoolihan leans towards me. Her eyes are shining bright. I wonder if she's turning as bonkers as him. I want to get back to daft Maxie and barmy Molecular Marx.

"This is about George, Daniel," she explains.

"George?"

"Yes, dear George."

"So what did you think of him?" says Eden Marsh.

"I thought he was … OK, I suppose."

"Excellent. So you got on all right with him? You thought he kind of fitted in? Taking into account his own little quirks and imperfections, of course."

I think about George. Aye, he's weird, but is he weirder than the rest of us? And who am I to start talking about another lad to a weird bloke like this?

"He seemed fine," I say.

"Excellent!"

"But is he OK now?"

"Eh?"

"Well, he didn't look too good in the yard at lunchtime."

Eden Marsh waves his hand in the air.

"Ah, don't worry about our George. He'll be as right as rain. A little glitch, that's all. A little bit of care and attention and he'll be as good as ever. *Better* than ever!"

He puts a sweet look on his face like I'm a little stupid kid.

"But thank you for your concern, Daniel," he adds. "I am very touched."

"Me, too," says Mrs Hoolihan.

"Just goes to show we're looking at the right lad, doesn't it, Mrs Hoolihan?"

"It does indeed, Mr Marsh."

He narrows his eyes and goes all man to man.

"The thing is, Daniel," he says to me, "we're looking for somebody who'll be George's pal when he comes back tomorrow."

"His pal?"

"Yep. Somebody to be at his side when he's here in school. And…"

He takes a deep breath.

"And how about this, Daniel? We're looking for somebody to take him home for tea."

Mrs Hoolihan is now trembling with excitement.

"What's the big fuss?" I want to say. "What's so special about taking somebody home for tea?"

"We want George," says Eden Marsh, in a very serious voice, "to experience an ordinary normal home with ordinary normal – and, OK, imperfect and quirky – folk in it. What do you think?"

I don't know what to think.

"You have a nice mum, I believe?" he says.

I don't say anything. Course I've got a nice mam.

"And what could be more normal?" he continues. "A nice lad and a nice mum in a nice home. Perfect. No dad, of course, but what's that these days? That in itself is very normal, is it not?"

Course there's no dad. He went off as soon as he found out I was being born. Never been heard of since. Good riddance, me and my mam always say.

Marsh looks at me, waits for me to answer.

"Aye," I mutter. "It is."

"So do you think your mam would be OK with that?" says Mrs Hoolihan. "I'm sure your lovely mam would be OK with that, wouldn't she?"

I shrug and mutter aye. They're both being so weird.

"He doesn't eat much," says Eden Marsh very quickly. "Doesn't drink too much, either. We've made your mam a little list of what he can and can't have."

"The food is unimportant," says Mrs Hoolihan. "The true purpose of the visit is to help George with his social skills. Is it not, Mr Marsh?"

"It is," agrees Eden Marsh. "So how about taking him home for tea tomorrow?"

"OK."

"Maybe you should phone your mam," says Mrs Hoolihan.

Straight away she's holding out her phone to me. I take it. I dial my mam's number. She's at work in her salon, *The New You.*

"Hello, Mam," I say when she answers.

"Hello, son. Everything OK?"

"Aye. Can I bring a friend for tea tomorrow?"

"Course you can, love."

"He's called George. He's a new kid."

"Oh, that's lovely."

"Seems he doesn't eat much."

"Ah, well. We'll make sure he has a nice time, son. Now, I've got to go. Got to finish Mrs Muldoon's nails."

"OK, Mam." I hand the phone back. "It's fine," I say.

"We're very grateful, Daniel," says Eden Marsh. "We've written a little note for your mum. To go with the list. So she'll know the kind of thing we're looking for."

He passes me an envelope. I put it in my pocket. "OK," I say.

"You won't understand now," says Eden Marsh. "But these events, and your part in them, Daniel, will go down in history."

12

I tell Maxie about it as we're walking home through the estate. He says it'll be great to get George on his own, away from all the weirdos. He says he's been thinking about things and he's decided that all kids are aliens; it's just we don't know it.

"All of us?" I say.

"Aye."

"So how do we not know it?" I say.

"Cos the memories have been wiped from our brains."

"Who by?"

"By teachers and mad scientists, politicians, people like that."

"But what about our parents? They would know, wouldn't they?"

"Aye, I did wonder. Then I thought they must've been brainwashed as well, so they can't remember where we really came from and who we really are."

"Brainwashed? Who by?"

"By the same people: politicians and teachers and mad scientists."

"Oh," I say.

"Stands to reason, doesn't it?" he says.

"Does it?"

"Aye. You know when you feel like you're dying for something, like yearning for it, and you can't put your finger on what it is you're dying for?"

"Aye," I say.

"Aye. That's the lost memory of our true planet shifting about inside us."

"Is it?"

"Aye. It's like we're all aching to get back to our proper home."

"Back to the planet we came from?"

"Aye. Stands to reason, doesn't it?"

I shrug.

"Aye, Maxie," I say. "It does."

It's Maxie, isn't it? Best just to let him ramble on.

We stop at Wilf's Corner Shop and Maxie buys a bag of cheese and onion crisps. I get prawn cocktail. We do that thing where we stuff the whole bagful of crisps into our mouths so they're so full we can hardly chew. Then we do chew, and we swallow the crisps and we sigh because they're so delicious.

"Prawn cocktail crisps, the finest in the universe," I say.

"Nah," says Maxie. "Cheese and onion for eternity."

We pass the Green Man pub and Hanlan's pie shop. We come to Mam's new beauty salon. *THE NEW YOU* is printed in Day-glo colours above the window. *!DISCOVER THE NEW YOU!* is painted across the glass. *!HAIR, NAILS, MAKE-UP, SKIN. WE DO IT ALL! !MAKEOVERS A SPECIALITY!*

I see Mam inside. She's sitting with a woman with green hair, doing her nails. She looks really happy, like she always does when she's at work. She sees us and waves. I wave back and we walk on.

We get to the big patch of grass with the cherry tree in the middle. One of the narrow tracks to Cogan's Wood starts from here. We can see the treetops beyond the rooftops.

"Coming out tonight?" I say.

"Nah. She's got the vicar coming round."

"The vicar?"

"Aye. He's coming for dinner and I've got to be there."

"What for?"

"Search me."

I wave goodbye and head homewards. I get my key and let myself in the back door. I put the kettle on and start cutting into a loaf of bread. I get the jam out of the fridge. Koshka comes in through the cat flap.

"Hiya, Kosh," I say.

I eat the bread and jam and have a cup of tea. Then I go upstairs to my room. Koshka comes with me. I sit on the bed with him on my lap and he purrs.

I lift my pillow and pull Ted out. Mam made him when I was a baby. He's knitted wool stuffed with padding that's almost disappeared from his arms and legs so he's all limp and floppy. He's got blue buttons for eyes. I used to do shows for Mam with Ted, get him to do lots of voices. We acted out daft plays. She thought it was hilarious.

He's always been my pal. He always knows what to say.

"Hi, Ted," I say.

"*Hi, Dan,*" I make him say back.

"You have a good day?" I say.

"*Aye, very canny. Went for a nice long walk. Made a new mate, another ted from Wincup Way.*"

"That's good. I've got a new mate and all. Name of George."

"*That's good. Is he nice?*"

"Aye. He is strange, though."

"*Strange?*"

"Aye. Almost like he's a..."

"*A what?*"

"I dunno, mate. He cannot be."

"*Cannot be what?*"

I groan. I don't know how to say it. It just sounds crackers.

"An … alien or something, or a—"

"*An alien?*"

"Aye, or even a… I know. It's mad. Anyway, I'm bringing him home to meet you tomorrow."

"*That's great, Dan.*"

I stroke Koshka. He purrs. I get my phone and call Maxie. I want to talk about George, but Maxie's all distracted. The vicar's already there. The new woman's talking about getting them all born again.

"Born *again?*" I say.

"Aye. Seems once is not enough."

I hear her calling for him.

"Maximilian! Come here now, please. You can talk to your friends any time. This is *important!*"

After a while Mam comes in from work. I go down to see her.

"Good day?" she says.

"Aye, Mam. Not bad. I've got a note for you about George."

She opens the envelope and reads the note.

"Certainly doesn't eat much, does he? *A few*

81

drops of olive oil. A small glass of water. A small piece
of dry bread or cake. No salt. Nothing sticky. Nothing
hot. That's not going to feed the lad up, is it?"

"No, Mam."

"Listen to this. *We wish you just to be an
ordinary normal little family. Do not make any special
arrangements. We would like George to be with you
for an hour or so. Then we will take him away.* What
does that mean? Ordinary? Normal?"

I shrug.

"Dunno. They're all being weird about it."

"Mebbe we can squeeze a bit of something else into him."

"Mebbe. We could try."

"Anyway, what's he like, this George?"

"I think he's got some sort of condition. Or he's been away or something."

"Has he got a family, or a mam and dad?"

"Dunno, Mam. I know nowt."

She laughs.

"Ah, well. We're good at looking after the waifs and strays, aren't we?"

She strokes Koshka's back. She strokes my head. She says she'll sort some tea out.

"*Ordinary*," she says again. "What does *that* mean?"

"Dunno, Mam."

"It's weird, eh?"

"Aye, Mam. Weird."

13

Next morning, the black van turns up at the school gates. George and Miss Crystal get out. George is wearing brand-new jeans and a red shirt and bright new blue and red trainers. He's smiling. Miss Crystal is in a blue flowery dress. She's got her black bag and she's smiling sweetly as always. They move through the kids in the yard towards the school entrance. George is walking easily, swinging his arms back and forward. He looks much better than he did last time we saw him.

Mrs Hoolihan hurries out to welcome them. Me and Maxie are standing close by.

"Good morning, George!" says Mrs Hoolihan.

"Good morning, Mrs Hoolihan," says George. He's got this weird fixed smile on his face.

"Welcome back to Darwin Avenue!" she says. "And how are you today, George?"

"I am perfectly splendid, thank you very much indeed," he says.

"Delighted to hear it, lad!"

Miss Crystal whispers something into George's ear. He suddenly turns and looks at everyone around him.

"Good morning, dear schoolmates!" he says. His voice is a bit louder than yesterday, a bit more confident.

"Well done, George," says Miss Crystal.

The Reception class fairies giggle together.

"Say it again, George!" one of them squeaks.

"Go on, George," says another.

Miss Crystal whispers again.

George stands up straighter. "Good morning, dear schoolmates."

The fairies squeak with delight.

Mrs Hoolihan guides him and Miss Crystal to the door.

I look back and see Eden Marsh leaning out of the van. He gives me a wave and a thumbs up. I turn away from him and watch George, Miss Crystal and Mrs Hoolihan go inside.

"I am perfectly splendid, thank you very much indeed!" says one of the fairies.

"Good morning, dear schoolmates!" says another.

They turn it into a little chant and they dance away together. They keep stopping to hug each other and giggle.

"How was the vicar?" I say to Maxie.

He pulls a face.

"Don't ask."

"OK."

"He says we could do it down in the river."

"Do what?"

"Get born again. Sounds like there's a bunch of people doing it. They go down to the river, strip off, jump in, jump out, and they're born again into a new life."

"What does your dad think?"

"Nowt much. But the vicar asked him if he was ready to be prepared for glory and he said aye, he supposed he was."

"And what about you?"

"Me? You're joking. I'm happy enough with this life. I'm happy enough being me."

Then the bell goes, and we start lining up. We start trooping into school. The teachers tell us

86

to keep in line so we keep in line. They tell us to keep our voices down so we keep our voices down. We head through the corridors to the classrooms. There's no assembly today. We go to our square tables. George is already in the classroom and sitting at our table. He's still smiling.

"Hiya, George," I say.

"Good morning, dear classmate," he says.

I take a quick look at his ear and it seems perfectly fine.

Mr Sage calls out our names and we say, "Here, Mr Sage. Good morning, Mr Sage."

He calls, "George One."

George says, "Here, Mr Sage. Good morning, Mr Sage."

"George One?" I say to George. "Is that your name?"

He looks at me.

"Good morning, dear classmate," he says.

George ONE? I mouth at Maxie.

He shrugs. *George One. So what?* He's got other stuff to worry about.

"Now let's get these minds working," says Mr Sage.

Billy groans. We do mental maths again. George gets all the impossible questions right again.

At the end of that, when Mr Sage has set us to do some quiet writing, Miss Crystal comes and sits down beside me. She smells of perfume. Her teeth are dazzling white.

"Thank you very much," she says softly, "for inviting George to tea."

"That's OK."

"I think we should have a little chat at break time," she says. "Just to sort the ins and outs of it all. Me and you and George."

"OK," I say.

I look at George. His pen's belting across his notebook.

At break time, I stay in the classroom with George, Miss Crystal and Mr Sage.

"This is the boy I told you about," says Miss Crystal to George. "His name is Daniel."

He looks at me like he's never seen me in his life before. I look at how smooth his skin is, how perfect his pale hair is.

"You met him yesterday," says Miss Crystal. "He sits at your table. He is your friend."

George blinks.

"A friend," he says, "is a person you enjoy being with. A friend is a person with whom you feel safe. A friend is someone with whom you can share confidences."

Mr Sage claps.

"That's *right*, George. Excellent, George. It shows great understanding, doesn't it, Miss Crystal?"

Miss Crystal looks at Mr Sage.

"Yes," she says. "It does."

She turns back to George.

"And Daniel," she says, "is the boy who is taking you home for tea. Say thank you, Daniel."

George blinks.

"Thank you, Daniel," he says. His lips hardly move. His eyes are turned towards me but it's like he's not looking at me.

"A friend," he says, "is someone with whom you can chew the fat. Tea is a drink made from water and the leaves of a plant grown in tropical regions, for example in the country named India."

"That's *right*, George," says Mr Sage.

He taps him on the shoulder.

"You're really coming on, lad. Keep it up."

Miss Crystal frowns and scribbles something down.

"Thanks, Dan," Mr Sage says to me. "Knew we could rely on you, lad. You've got the right pal here, George."

I look out into the yard where all the kids are playing and messing about in the sunshine. I see how scruffy some of us are, how wild some of us must seem.

"You have seen the list," says Miss Crystal, "of what George can and cannot eat and drink?"

"Yes."

"And your mother's happy with it?"

"Suppose so."

"Good. I'll be coming along too," she says.

"You?"

"But at a distance. I just need to keep an eye on the young man, to maintain a record of his condition and his movements. He can't be left alone, not yet. But don't worry. I don't need to be catered for."

"OK," I mutter.

"And at lunchtime today," says Miss Crystal, and she grins and widens her eyes, "as a further part of George's development, we would like to give him the opportunity to play football."

"That's brilliant!" I say, and I mean it. I grin across at him. "You'll love it."

"Football is…" George begins, but the bell's ringing and it's time for lessons again.

14

At lunchtime we go onto the pitch and pick sides. I say that George should be on my team today and everybody says OK.

I stand with him in the middle of the pitch.

"You're on my side," I tell him. "You'll be all right, mate."

He looks at me.

"You've played before, haven't you, George?" I ask.

He says nothing.

The game starts and kids rush at the ball. George doesn't move. He just stares into space.

I get the ball and start running at the goal. Somebody gets it off me and blasts it back upfield again. It flies past George's head. He still doesn't move. I see Miss Crystal at the pitchside scribbling notes.

Joe Link, on our team, passes the ball to George. It bounces straight past him. He doesn't move an inch.

"George!" yells Joe. "Come on, man! Get stuck in!"

Joe glares at me.

"What's wrong with him? I thought he *wanted* to play."

"So did I, Joe."

Matilda Fernandez from the other side gets the ball and dribbles round George. She does it again. He doesn't move. She runs on and blasts it into the goal.

"Goaaaal!" she screams.

"George!" yells a kid from our side. "You should have tackled her, man!"

He doesn't flinch.

I get the ball for kick-off. I stand beside George.

"We're one-nil down," I say. He still doesn't flinch. "We have to score."

I roll the ball and it touches his foot.

Suddenly George drops his shoulder, knocks the ball to the side and sets off running with it at his feet. Kids from the other team rush after him; he swerves past them all. He turns and swerves past them all again. They can't get the ball off him. He's so fast; he's so clever. Sometimes he looks like he's just about to lose it, but it's a trick. He drags the ball back again.

Now there's a whole bunch of kids from the other side storming around him.

"**Pass it!**" yells Joe.

"**Pass it, George! Pass it!**" we all shout.

He flicks the ball up onto his knee, knocks it over his head, traps it with his heel. He feints, swerves, shimmies.

"**Pass it, George!**"

"**Over here, George!**"

"**On me head, George!**"

He breaks free of the group and runs full speed at the goal. He lashes the ball into the corner of the net from twenty yards.

We go mad. We've never seen anything like it. We all jump around him, slapping him on the shoulder and grinning.

"That was amazing, George!" I tell him.

"Where the hell did you learn how to play like that?" asks Maxie.

George says nothing. He stands dead still and stares into space as if nothing has happened.

We start the game again.

"Give it to George!" we yell.

The ball flies over him and he doesn't move. It bounces past him and he doesn't move. Then it touches his foot and he controls it fast and he's off again. One man against the whole team. He beats them all. They can't do anything about it.

He blasts the ball into the net again. I run to him and clap him on the back.

"That was brilliant, mate!"

He stares at me. He's not out of breath at all.

"You could try passing it sometimes, though," I say.

I see Miss Crystal writing. She's smiling.

"Are you OK?" I say to George.

"I am perfectly splendid, thank you very much indeed."

The game starts again and George scores another goal just as amazing as the others. Then the bell goes and we have to stop.

Maxie comes over and we head back inside with George.

"That was fantastic, mate," Maxie says.

George pauses and blinks. He looks at me and Maxie with his pale blue eyes.

"Thanks, mate," he says.

15

Straight after lunch we have music with Mrs Imani in the school hall, after the tables have been cleared away. She smiles at us all and gives a particular smile and wave to George, who's standing at my side.

"Hello, George," she says. "It's so lovely to have you with us today!"

She looks over at Miss Crystal, who's sitting at the side of the hall with her notebook.

"And hello, Miss Crystal," she says. "I hope you'll be joining in too."

Miss Crystal frowns and looks down.

Mrs Imani's great. She's full of energy. All the kids like her, even the ones who aren't really that keen on music, even the ones who think she's a bit mad. She says that music is life itself. She makes us all feel we can sing. She even makes us all feel we can dance. She tells us to let the music come into us, and let the music flow out of us. She tells us music is natural. It's what human beings have been doing since the beginning of human time. We did it in ancient caves and we're doing it in a school hall today.

When she first came, Billy Dodds wouldn't sing at all. Then when he did try he just kind of grunted, so she got him to sing a song called "Deep River". She said it was a song for bass voices so he could sing it just as if it was a groan. He squirmed and blushed, but he did get going, very slowly, which was dead right, she said, because it can be a very slow song.

"Dee-eep river,
My home is over Jordan.
Dee-eep river, Lord.
I want to cross over into campground."

She got us all to join in, and we did. We swayed and sang, with Billy Dodds at the heart of us, and you could tell it made Billy happy. From then on, he loved his music lessons more than any others. And so did most of the rest of us.

We've been practising a song from Ghana called "Tue Tue". We all like it. The tune and the words are

easy. Mrs Imani sings
it now to remind us.

"*Tue tue barima tue tue*
Abofra ba
Ama wa da wa
Tue tue.
It's just so simple,
isn't it?" she says.

"Yes," we say.

"But then think of all the complex movements
and harmonies we've been creating around the
simplicity."

It's true. We've been using drums and clappers
and tambourines, and we've been working hard to
make the whole thing big and relaxed and beautiful,
and some of us sing soft and some of us sing loud,
but all of us kind of get lost in it.

"It's simple like a human being, isn't it?" she says.

"What do you mean, Miss?" asks Louise.

"Well, we're all dead simple, aren't we? Each one of us is pretty much the same. We're all made to the same pattern: two legs, two arms, a body and a head."

We all look around at one another. Yes, the simple pattern is everywhere. I look at George, my strange new pal: two legs, two arms, a body and a head.

"But at the same time, we're all so different, aren't we?" said Mrs Imani. "Dead simple, but what variety, what complexity, what mystery!"

She laughs.

"We are a room full of very mysterious creatures!"

We all laugh.

"And now, my weird creatures," says Mrs Imani, "let us prepare to sing!"

We get out the drums and clappers and tambourines. I take a drum for myself. We get into our groups. I make sure George is with me and Maxie.

"You won't know the words yet, George," says Mrs Imani. "But you'll pick it all up, I'm sure."

She tells us to breathe, to shake our hands and feet, to stretch our mouths wide, to bare our teeth, to waggle our tongues. She tells us to let the musical energy into ourselves.

"Can you feel it?" she asks.

"Yes," we tell her; and yes, we can. And she gives us a note, and off we go.

We sing; we sway; we beat our drums and shake our tambourines.

"Tue tue barima tue tue
Abofra ba
Ama wa da wa
Tue tue."

The words mean "Sorry, man, sorry. This little boy has made you fall flat on your face. Sorry. Sorry."

Maybe it'd look a bit weird to somebody who just came and stared in at the window at us. We'd look like a pack of ancient folk in an ancient cave.

George doesn't sing and he doesn't move. I tap the drum, beat the drum. I hold it towards him, so he can feel its vibrations.

At the end, Mrs Imani tells us how wonderful we are. She suggests how we could improve it even further, and she asks some of us to sing again.

She shows us how to strengthen it, to deepen it, to sweeten it. She moves through the group to George.

"Don't worry. You'll pick up the words, George. Do you like singing?"

No answer.

"We'll find a song that fits you, just like we did with Billy. And then you won't look back. Would you like me to help you with this one?"

No answer.

She sings the first line of the song softly.

"Tue tue barima tue tue…"

George tilts his head and seems to listen. She sings it again.

"Now you, George," she whispers.

"Go on, mate," I tell him.

He opens his mouth. He does try to sing.

"Tue tue barima tue tue…"

He gets the words right, but he can't do the tune. The words come out flat, in a straight line, just like his writing.

Mrs Imani tries again. George tries again. But it's just the same.

"Don't worry, George," she says. "You will be fine."

George tries again.

"*Tue tue barima tue tue…*"

Billy Dodds comes over to stand with us.

"I'll sing it with you, mate," he says.

Billy sings. George tries to sing. It's just the same.

"Don't worry," says Billy. "It'll come, just like it did with me."

Miss Crystal scribbles.

George tries again. Mrs Imani smiles.

"One day you will sing, George," she says, "and it will be beautiful."

George says nothing.

"Oh, dear George," she says, and there are tears in her eyes.

16

"Why're they always watching him?" Maxie says as we're leaving school that day.

"Beats me," I say.

We've come out of the school gates. I've got Maxie on one side of me, George on the other.

"Why're they always watching you?" Maxie asks George.

George says nothing, just walks with us, eyes looking straight ahead.

Miss Crystal is a few yards behind.

A hundred yards behind her, the black van has come out of a side street and has started to follow us. It's moving dead slowly, and gleaming in the bright sunlight.

We keep on walking. We come to the patch of grass with the cherry tree growing on it. Under the tree, we pause.

"Do you never want to just run away from them?" asks Maxie.

George says nothing.

Maxie steps round me so we make a kind of triangle, me, George and Maxie in a tight group, heads and bodies close together beneath the tree. There's lots of kids around, heading home from school or just hanging about the estate. Some of them wave at us and call George's name. But we do that thing that mates can do where it seems we're on our own.

"You can tell us what's going on," says Maxie. "We'll not tell anybody."

George doesn't answer.

"Have you got other mates?" I say. "At home or somewhere?"

No answer.

I glance back and see Miss Crystal scribbling in her notebook.

"Or any family?" says Maxie.

"A family is—" starts George.

"Aye," I cut in. "We know what it is, George. But what about *your* family? What about your mam and dad? What about your home?"

He just stares back at us, like he understands

none of this. I touch his arm. I look into his eyes, so blue, so still.

"What *are* you, George?" I say.

No answer.

Miss Crystal is coming slowly closer. I want to tell her to get lost, to stop spying and prying. I point to the narrow pathway between the houses.

"That's where Cogan's Wood is," I tell him. "And freedom."

Miss Crystal's very close. We move on from the tree; we pass the pale pebble-dashed houses, the black roadways, the kids playing in their little square gardens and on their verges. A couple of dogs run past.

"These are animals," says George.

"Aye," I say. "Dogs."

"These are houses. These are trees. These are children."

"Yes," I say. "Well done, George."

"There are birds in the sky. The sky is blue."

"Yes," says Maxie.

We get to Wilf's Corner Shop. Maxie goes in and comes out with a bag of cheese and onion and a bag of prawn cocktail. We start stuffing them in.

"Wanna crisp?" Maxie mumbles to George.

"Don't think he can," I say.

"Huh. Course he can."

He holds a crisp out to George and George opens his mouth and sticks his tongue out, and Maxie puts the crisp on George's tongue. George closes his mouth. Maxie grins.

"Blimmin' delicious, eh?" he says.

But suddenly Miss Crystal's here.

"Open your mouth, George!" she orders.

She touches his lips and pushes them apart.

"Spit it out!"

He just stares and lets her reach into his mouth. She fiddles in there with her fingers and pulls out fragments of cheese and onion crisp. She flicks and scatters them onto the ground.

"You have seen the list!" she snaps. "You know he can't have such things."

"What harm—" begins Maxie.

She takes a deep breath.

"Boys," she says. "You do not *understand*."

"Understand *what*?" I say.

"Understand George. Understand what he is; how important he is."

"Tell us, then," says Maxie.

She takes another deep breath.

108

"All I can tell you is that George is very special," she says. "And he has a very delicate constitution. And we must look after him. You do want to look after him, don't you?"

"Yes," I tell her.

"Course we do," says Maxie. "He's our mate."

"Good. That is what we must all strive to do."

She reaches into George's mouth again.

"All gone, I think," she says. "No harm done, I hope."

She scribbles in her notebook. She smooths her dress down; she smooths George's hair.

"George is not like other boys," she says.

She looks at each of us in turn.

"George is not like *you*. That is what we must all remember."

We stare back at her, then we move on.

She follows again.

"Don't worry, George," whispers Maxie. "You *are* like us."

We keep on walking.

"Aye," I say. "Whatever you are, you are like us. You're one of us."

I feel George lean against me for a moment.

"You are Daniel," he says.

"Yes," I say.

"And I'm Maxie," says Maxie.

"You are Maxie," says George. "You are Daniel."

"And you are George," I say.

No answer. I'm about to say more, but here's Miss Crystal again.

"Are we almost there?" she says. "We must be almost there."

"We are," I tell her.

She smiles at Maxie.

"So you'll be heading to your own home now, will you, Maximilian?"

"Aye," answers Maxie. "I will."

He rolls his eyes and gives me a high five. George watches. Maxie lifts George's hand and shows George how to do it. George tries a couple of times, then he gets it. He slaps Maxie's hand in mid-air. Maxie grins.

"See you, mates," he says, then he's gone.

17

My mam's great. She's got everything ready on the kitchen table. Cups and saucers and plates. There's some cheese sandwiches, and a lemon cake, my favourite. There's a jug of water and a small bottle of olive oil. There's a little vase of flowers from the garden.

"Hello!" she calls as we go in. "And this must be George. Hello, son, make yourself at home."

I guide George to a chair and he sits there, not moving, not speaking.

"So how are you, lad?" Mam says to him. "Enjoying your first days at your new school?"

"I am perfectly splendid, thank you very much indeed," says George.

Mam beams.

"What politeness! But no need to stand on ceremony. I know what you lads are!"

She turns to Miss Crystal.

"Now then, pet," she says. "Welcome to you, too."

"I am Miss Crystal," says Miss Crystal. "Take no notice of me."

Mam blinks.

"Take no notice of you? How do I do that?"

Miss Crystal doesn't answer. She smiles her sweet smile and backs into a corner and stands there with her notebook and pen in her hands.

"At least have a seat," says Mam. "Can't have you standing there like a lummock while we're sitting here tucking in, can we?"

She pushes a chair towards Miss Crystal, who takes it and sits down.

"Will you at least have a cup of tea?"

Miss Crystal shakes her head.

"No, thank you. Imagine I'm not here. Just get on with things in a normal ordinary manner if you would."

Mam shrugs. She laughs.

"Now then, George," she says. "I don't know *how* to behave now I've been told to be normal. Normal, ordinary. How do I do that? I like your shirt. Lovely jeans as well. Very smart! Oh look, here's our Koshka come to see you!"

Koshka comes in through the cat flap. Miss Crystal flinches.

"A cat!" she says.

"Our Koshka," says Mam. "Isn't he lovely?"

"We didn't know about that," says Miss Crystal. "George is not used to animals."

"He'll be OK with our Kosh," Mam assures her.

Miss Crystal scribbles something down.

Koshka jumps up onto George's lap, then lies there and starts to purr.

"Give him a stroke, George," says Mam.

George does nothing. Mam smiles at him. "Not used to animals, eh? I can see that."

She takes his hand and moves it gently across

Koshka's fur. She moves her hand away and George keeps stroking.

"That's right, George," says Mam. "Very good. You've got a pal for life there, now."

George gazes down at the cat and at his hand moving over the cat.

Miss Crystal watches him and scribbles in her notebook.

"George played football today," I say.

"Football!" says Mam.

"Aye. He was brilliant. Weren't you, George?"

He turns his eyes from Koshka to me.

"Football," I say. "Remember?"

He says nothing. I can see how confused Mam is.

"I know!" she says. "Would you like Dan to take you up to his room for a bit before tea? That'd be nice, wouldn't it?"

She nods at me. *Go on.*

"Aye," I say. "Good idea." I stand up. "Howay, George." I touch his arm.

Miss Crystal stands up too.

"You're going as well?" says Mam.

"Yes, please," says Miss Crystal. "I have to record everything."

Mam shrugs, but I can see she's wondering what the hell is going on.

I lift Koshka off George's lap and head upstairs with George and Miss Crystal and Koshka following close behind.

"That's very good," says Mam. "That looks very ordinary."

We go into my room. I sit on the bed and get George to sit beside me. Miss Crystal stands in the corner watching and scribbling. Koshka jumps up onto George's lap again. George starts to stroke him. I reach under the pillow for Ted.

"This is Ted," I say to George. "Say hello to George, Ted."

"Hello, George," I make Ted say in a deep voice.

George says nothing.

I turn Ted towards Miss Crystal.

"Hello, Miss Crystal," I make Ted say.

Miss Crystal says nothing. Ted keeps looking at her. She doesn't look very pleased. We all stay like that in silence for a while. George strokes the cat. He strokes Ted.

"This is my bedroom," I explain to George. "It's been my bedroom since I was born."

I laugh.

"Once I was a tiny baby sleeping in a cot here. I can hardly remember that. Then I was a little boy in a little bed and I *can* remember that. Now I'm me in here with you, and one day I'll remember that, too."

George strokes Koshka and Ted.

"Ted's been with me from the very start," I say. "Koshka came when I was three."

"Kosh-ka," says George.

"That's right. Koshka. Ted."

"Kosh-ka. Ted."

Miss Crystal writes.

"Do you have a room like this?" I say.

George just looks at me.

I want to ask him everything, but I don't know how to start. And it's so weird and so stupid, with somebody writing down everything we do and say. I want to tell her to get out of my room, to stop spying and prying. I want to tell her this is my place

117

and I want it to be just me and George. "What *are* you, George?" I say to him.

No answer.

Miss Crystal just scribbles. She gives a soft laugh.

"Who *made* you, George?" I say.

Miss Crystal stops scribbling. She stares at me.

"Who *made* him?" I say to her.

She shakes her head and sniggers. I stare at her. She's so dry, so cold, not like a human being at all.

"Who?" I say. "Who made him? Who created him?"

"What a very silly question," she says.

"Is it?"

"Yes. And such a waste of our time. We only have an hour or so. We must go back down."

She whispers in George's ear. He puts Ted and Koshka down on the bed and stands up.

"Well done, George," says Miss Crystal.

We go back down.

"Welcome back," says Mam. "You lads must be starving. Now then, George, I'm told that a cheese sandwich might not be the thing."

"No indeed!" says Miss Crystal quickly.

Mam ignores her.

"But I believe a little bit of this cake might be in order."

"Ahem," says Miss Crystal. "Not sticky cake, is it?" She peers at the cake.

"Dry as dust," confirms Mam, "as per the instructions. Dry and sweet and quite delicious."

She cuts a little piece and holds it out to George. George opens his mouth, sticks his tongue out, and Mam puts a fragment of cake on it. He closes his mouth.

"And now a couple of drops of olive oil if you would," says Miss Crystal.

"Now?" says Mam.

"Yes," says Miss Crystal. "Please. Two or three drops on his tongue to help the process."

Mam pours a couple of drops of the olive oil onto a spoon, but she can't help herself.

"I've got to say," she says, "that I find this all a bit odd. Doesn't a lad of George's age need something a bit more—"

"These are the instructions," says Miss Crystal. "This is what will keep George well."

"It's all a bit beyond me," admits Mam.

She tips the drops onto George's tongue. She looks into his eyes.

"Do you *like* that, George?" she says.

"I am perfectly splendid, thank you very much indeed," says George.

"That's very good to know," says Mam.

I bite into a cheese sandwich. It's lovely. Mam looks at me. *What on earth is going on?* her eyes say.

Koshka leaps onto George's lap.

George runs his hand across his fur, and Koshka purrs.

"Ah, he loves that," says Mam. "He knows a good lad when he sees one."

Miss Crystal scribbles. George keeps running his hand across Koshka's fur.

Koshka keeps on purring.

The afternoon sun streams through the kitchen window. I eat my sandwich. Mam pours tea for her and me.

"It's a lovely day, isn't it?" Mam says to George.

No reply.

Mam sips.

"So..." she says, searching for something else to talk about. "Do you have a cat yourself, George? At your own home or...?"

"He won't answer that," says Miss Crystal.

"Can he not speak for himself, Miss Crystal?"

"He *can't* answer that, I should have said."

"*Can't?* Why ever not?"

"I can't tell you that," says Miss Crystal.

"There's a lot of not telling," says Mam, "isn't there?"

"I'm afraid there is," says Miss Crystal, smiling sweetly.

"Why is that?"

"There is much that is confidential."

"Confidential?"

"Perhaps I should say *classified*."

"Pardon?"

"I'm sorry. I can give you no more information.

But everything will be clarified before too long."

Mam reaches out and touches George's shoulder. He doesn't move.

I can see that she wants to stand up for him and help, but how can she talk about him when he can hardly talk himself, and when somebody like Miss Crystal is scribbling down everything anybody says?

"I know!" says Mam suddenly. "Maybe George would like to come for a sleepover."

"A sleepover?" says Miss Crystal. "That would, I'm afraid, be out of the—"

"Yes," says Mam. "That would be very ordinary and normal, wouldn't it, Daniel?"

"Aye! Just like when Maxie comes over. How about it, George? Maxie could come, too. There'd be the three of us! You could come over after school and we could—"

"No," says Miss Crystal. "That cannot be done."

"Why ever not?" says Mam again.

"George is not ready for such things."

"What do you mean he's not ready? He'd have a lovely time, wouldn't he, Dan?"

"Course he would," I say. "What do you think, George? I think we should sort it out, Mam."

122

George doesn't look at us. He keeps his eyes on Koshka.

Miss Crystal has her phone out and she is sending a text.

"Thank you very much for inviting George," she says, smiling. "It has been very valuable for him."

"And that's it?" says Mam.

"Yes. We said it would be just a short visit. You have been very accommodating."

"Accommodating?"

"Yes. Thank you. Now, George, it is time to go."

Through the window, I see the black van draw up in the street.

Miss Crystal takes George's arm and tries to get him to stand up. George keeps looking down at Koshka and stroking him.

"George," says Miss Crystal. "It is time to go."

"Look at him," says Mam. "He's having a lovely time. Can't he have a little longer?"

"It is for the best. I can see that George is finding this rather difficult."

She whispers into George's ear. He stands. Koshka jumps down to the floor.

"Thank you very much," says George. "Thank you very much indeed."

Miss Crystal leads him to the front door.

"George," I say. "Mate."

I follow him out of the door.

Miss Crystal leads him down the path. The driver's door of the van opens.

"George!" I say.

He pauses. He looks back at me.

"Mate," he says. He takes a step back from the van.

"No, George!" says Miss Crystal, gripping him firmly by the elbow.

Eden Marsh gets out of the van.

He walks past George and Miss Crystal and comes to stand before us at the door.

"Thank you so much, madam," he says to Mam, shaking her hand. "You have been most helpful."

"Is George all right?" says Mam.

"He is fine," says Marsh. "He is not yet perfect. But with the help of good folk like yourself, we will find a way to reach perfection."

"Perfection?"

Marsh smiles his handsome smile.

"Forgive me," he says. "I know how confusing this must be. But trust me. He is fine."

He laughs and looks back at George.

"Look at him," he says. "What a boy. What an achievement!"

He shakes Mam's hand again, then turns to me and lowers his voice. "You're a very perceptive lad," he says. "The assistance of you and your mother will go down in history."

He smiles. He leaves.

He and Miss Crystal guide George towards the van.

"No," says George. "No."

"Yes, George," says Marsh. "Get back in where you belong."

And he pushes George into the van.

"See you tomorrow, George!" I call.

But George doesn't answer. The van door slides shut, and he's gone.

18

Not long afterwards, I run through the streets of the estate to meet Maxie.

We go to the swings park and we sit on the bench at the side. Kids are swinging on the swings, sliding down the slide, climbing on the climbing frames. Everything ordinary, normal, the same as ever. Everything as it's always been and will always be. And everything weirder than ever.

"He's a robot," I say.

"Who is?" says Maxie.

"George, of course."

"*George?*"

"Aye. Or something like a robot. Or…"

"Or *what?*"

"I dunno, do I? But he's *something*."

"Everybody's something."

Maxie frowns and stares at the sky.

"A *robot?*" he says. "How do you work that out?"

"Just the way he goes on, the things he does."

"You're joking," he says. "It cannot be true."

"But mebbe it is. Mebbe it's the only possible answer."

He stares at the sky again.

"Have *you* not thought it?" I say.

"*Me?* I've got enough to think about with the new woman and getting born again."

"Well, think about it now. Think about the way he plays football, or the mental maths, or how he can hardly eat anything, and the way they keep watching him all the time, and his voice, and his ear, and…"

Maxie shakes his head.

"It's crackers, man. It's as barmy as saying we're all aliens."

"But you did say that!"

"Aye, but I didn't mean it."

"Didn't you?"

"No. Yes. It was just a way of thinking about what we might be."

"So think about what George might be, as well."

He frowns, he shrugs, he ponders.

"It cannot be true," he whispers. "*Can it?*"

We look at the kids on the swings. We look at
the estate, the place where we've grown up together.
A bunch of kids race past dressed as superheroes.
One of them yells that there's an earthquake in
Simpson Street and they've got to stop it fast.

"Hurry!" they yell. "Run! The city is being
destroyed!"

I tell Maxie about Koshka and Ted and the cake
and Eden Marsh coming to fetch George in the van.

"They wouldn't let him stay," I say. "They knew
I suspected what was going on. They had to get
him away from me."

"They're always doing that, aren't they? Watching him, making sure he doesn't get too close to us."

"It's cos he's a robot and they don't want us to find out yet."

"*Is* it? Is it *really?*"

"He called me mate," I say.

"Mate?"

"Aye. And they hated it. They don't want him to be our mate, not really."

"They're monsters," says Maxie.

"They are," I agree. "And it doesn't really matter if he's a kid or a robot or something even weirder. We've got to get him away from them."

Maxie clenches his fists and glares into space.

"He needs us, Maxie," I say. "We've got to save him."

"But *how?*"

"I dunno. Yes, I do! We'll take him to Cogan's Wood."

"Aye! Let's hide him there!"

"He'll be fine there," I say. "No matter what he is and no matter what's happened to him in the past."

"Brilliant!"

"We'll get him away from those monsters."

"Kidnap him!"

"Ha! That's it, kidnap him and save him!"

"How?"

"Ha. Somehow!"

"Somehow!"

We try to think about how we might do it. There's no answer.

"I don't know how," I say, "but we'll do it tomorrow."

"Tomorrow! Aye!"

We punch the air. We feel like we could do anything together. We always have. Me and Maxie. Maxie and me. Soon it'll be George and Maxie and me. Us and the new kid. The robot or whatever he is. Three of us, together.

"And tell nobody," I say. "Don't let them see how mad we are. Don't let anybody suspect anything."

"Tomorrow!" says Maxie.

"Aye! Tomorrow. We'll do it tomorrow, mate."

19

Tomorrow comes. Into school we go. Into our square rooms we go. But no sign of George. No van, no Miss Crystal, no Eden Marsh.

Now we're settled at our square tables, here's Mrs Hoolihan coming in. Her face is both sad and smiley.

"I am the bearer of sad news," she says. "I'm afraid that our friend George will not be joining us today."

"He will be coming back, though?" says Louise.

"Yes, dear," says Mrs Hoolihan. "In fact, we have arranged a special event for Friday, when George will return."

Mr Sage grins. He taps his cheek.

"He will return," he says like he's being oh so clever, "but perhaps in a different form…"

He fends away all our questions.

"You will just have to wait and see," he says.

I look at Maxie. I'm right. I know I'm right.

"Everybody is very pleased with George's time at our school," says Mrs Hoolihan. "Everyone is very grateful for all your assistance. You can all be very proud of yourselves."

"What have they done to him?" says Maxie.

"What have *who* done to him?" says Mrs Hoolihan.

"*Them.* That woman. That man. Those…"

"Oh, Maximilian, nobody has done anything. Who would do anything to lovely George? Who *could* do anything to a boy like George?"

"*They* could!" says Maxie. "Those *monsters!*"

"Oh, Maximilian."

"We know what he *is!*" says Maxie.

Mrs Hoolihan and Mr Sage stare at him.

"What on earth do you mean, dear?" says Mrs Hoolihan. "You know what he *is?*"

Maxie stands up. He looks across at me.

"We do, don't we, Dan? We've worked it out, haven't we?"

I glare back at him. I tell him with my eyes, *No! Don't let them know that we know. Don't let them see how mad we are. Or they might never bring him back.*

132

"What is the matter, Maximilian?" says Mr Sage.

Maxie shrugs. He shakes his head. He sees I'm right.

"Nothing," he says.

"He's our mate," I explain. "Just our mate."

"I see," says Mrs Hoolihan. "But maybe George is not capable of being anybody's mate."

"He is!" I say. "He even called me mate!"

She gazes at me sadly.

"You have such a big heart, Daniel. You're a credit to us all. I'm sure that George is as grateful to you as he can possibly be."

Mr Sage raises his hands, like he's in a state of wonder.

"You're such a lucky lot," he says. "To be alive at such momentous times. To see a brand-new world being brought to life before your very eyes."

"Yes indeed," says Mrs Hoolihan. "We here at Darwin Avenue Primary Academy are at the forefront, at the cutting edge."

She says she has to leave us now. Mr Sage says we must move on, and must turn our minds again to the discoveries and inventions which have changed the world.

He writes GREAT INVENTIONS on the blackboard.

He tells us to open our books.

He tells us to open our minds.

He tells us to make sure we are here on Friday.

He deepens his voice.

"And prepare," he says, "to be astonished."

20

We try to play football that lunchtime, but nobody can concentrate. No one can stop thinking about the mystery of the new kid. The mystery of George. Dev Hassan's a brilliant player and he tries to do some of the tricks that George did, but he can't do anything like them.

He tries again and fails again.

"What a player!" he says. "Messi and Ronaldo all in one!"

We all spend a moment seeing again in our minds George's wonderful play.

In the yard the Reception class fairies say how much they miss him.

They do a sad slow prance and dance.

"I am perfectly splendid, thank you very much indeed," they sadly chant.

"Good morning, dear schoolmates," they sadly say.

They shed a few sad tears.

"George!" they call, in their little high sad voices. "Come back to us soon, lovely George."

Even Nintendo Norah asks about him. She says he seemed a very canny lad.

Maxie and I are despondent at the end of the day as we walk back through the estate.

"Mebbe we've missed our chance to rescue him," he says. "On Friday they'll all be there. A *special event*. The monsters. The teachers."

I sigh. I know.

At the cherry tree, we pause. The blossom is bright above our heads. The hedges along the pathway to Cogan's Wood are growing fast.

Maxie's phone rings. He has to go. I wander on.

At home, Mam shakes her head when I tell her that George wasn't in today.

"Such a strange lad," she says. She kisses the top of my head. "He's never been properly loved. Not like you have."

"Has he not?"

"I could tell after just a few short minutes."

"You could have loved him, couldn't you, Mam?"

"Me? Course I could, son. Like any proper mam would do."

She hugs me tight.

"It's all anybody needs when they're young," she says. "To be properly loved, that's all."

Upstairs I get Ted out from under the pillow. Koshka comes in and sits with us on the bed. I tell them both about George.

"*I like him,*" says Ted. "*So does Koshka. Don't you, Koshka?*"

Koshka purrs.

I gaze out at the estate, at the birds flying through the empty sky above.

So strange. George was here less than two days. He hardly spoke. Nobody understood him. He was probably the weirdest boy any of us has ever come across. At one moment he seemed like the rest of us, and the next he was hardly like a boy at all.

Maybe he's not even human.

But he touched all of us.

And when he's not here, it's like he leaves a hole in all our lives.

21

Friday, last day of the Easter term. Nothing happens in the morning except the weird things we get up to every morning. At lunchtime me and Maxie wonder if they're not bringing George back at all. Maybe they've taken him to another school, we say. Maybe they've taken him back to wherever he started from.

We think about him falling down in the yard the other day.

"Maybe it's happened again," says Maxie. "Maybe he's finished. Maybe he's died."

Then lunchtime's over and we troop back into the classroom.

We're all looking forward to the holidays, but me and Maxie can't feel the excitement today.

"Where's George?" says Louise. "When are they coming back with him?"

"Soon," says Mr Sage. "I'm sure it'll be soon."

"I'm sure it'll be soon," mutters Billy. "Just the kind of thing they always say."

"These things don't always go to plan," says Mr Sage. "It's very, very complicated, Billy."

He tells us to take it easy. Read or write or draw. He's nervous. He keeps looking through the window towards the yard and the street outside. He keeps saying it'll be soon; it's very, very complicated.

Then he sighs and clenches his fists, and we all sit up.

Here it is, the black van, coming through the gates.

We move to the window.

The van pulls up beside the school garden.

Miss Crystal and Marsh get out and walk round to the back of the van.

Marsh opens it up.

Two burly blokes get out, and carefully lift something behind them. It's a tall rectangular white box. It has **FRAGILE** printed on it. It has **THIS WAY UP** printed on it.

My heart sinks. *Thud*. It can't be. Can it?

Maxie's at my side.

"It can't be," he whispers. "Can it?"

140

We just look at each other.

"Dunno," I whisper.

"Where's George?" says Louise to Mr Sage.

He shakes his head.

"Just wait," he says. He tugs his collar, loosens his tie. He looks even more nervous.

"Where is he?" says Louise again.

Mr Sage can't look her in the eye.

"Just wait," he repeats. "We'll all find out soon."

"When?"

"When it's time, Louise. When everything is prepared. We have to wait until we're called."

Billy snarls. He looks at me and Maxie.

"What? Until we're called? Do they think they own us?"

The burly blokes set the box down on the ground. Then they get a red trolley out and lift the box onto it.

Marsh nods at them and they carefully wheel the box towards the school entrance.

He spots us all at the windows. He smiles and waves, like we must be so happy to see him again.

The burly blokes and Marsh and Miss Crystal and the box all enter the school.

"Sit back down now," says Mr Sage.

He tries to sound all cheery.

"Could be we'll be let off early today! Why not take the chance to get your bags packed for the hols."

My heart's thumping. My hands are shaking. We get our stuff out of drawers and off shelves. Maxie stuffs his boots and books into his sports bag. I do the same. I zip my drum into my drum bag.

Billy checks he's got his gardening tools together

in his gardening bag. Louise cleans her violin and slips it into its case.

I get a book out but I can't read. I get a notebook out but I can't write. I scribble a drawing of Cogan's Wood with me and Maxie and George walking through it. It's like looking at a dream, a useless dream.

And after a time the classroom door opens. Maureen Miller comes in and whispers in Mr Sage's ear, and he takes a deep breath, and he beams at us all.

"Yes," he says. "At last we have been called."

22

They're at the front, sitting on chairs facing us, looking oh so pleased with themselves and oh so important. Miss Crystal and Eden Marsh and the two burly blokes.

They've got the big white box sitting beside them on the trolley.

FRAGILE. THIS WAY UP.

There's a table there as well.

There's fewer kids than normal. It's just the older classes. No Reception class, no infant lasses, no fairies.

Some of the teachers sit at the sides: Mr Sage, Mrs Imani, Molecular Marx.

Mrs Hoolihan comes to the front.

"As you will see," she says, "the event is only for you older ones, for you special ones."

"Why's that?" calls someone.

"We feel that the younger ones might not be able to understand."

"Where's George?" calls someone else.

"Yeah, where's George?"

"Where is he?"

"Where's George, Miss?"

Mrs Hoolihan says we must wait a little longer. Everything will be revealed, she says. She beckons us forward. We move as she asks, closer to the front. We sit down on the floor. There's much muttering and wondering.

I can see that other kids are thinking the same as me.

I can't take my eyes off the box, can't help picturing what might be inside.

"Let us begin as we always begin," says Mrs Hoolihan. "Let us lift up our hearts and sing!"

She waves at Mr McKenna and he starts banging away at the piano.

"All things bright and beautiful,
All creatures great and small,
All things wise and wonderful,
The Lord God made them all."

But the singing isn't bright and beautiful. There's no Mrs Imani orchestra. Everybody's waiting, wondering. Me and Maxie don't do that thing where we sing as we're breathing in, so we sound like ghosts or like we're about to croak. We don't sing at all. We look at the adults, at the big white box. I look at the teachers and some of them aren't singing either. Even Mrs Imani doesn't sing. She stares at the box. Molecular Marx is dead serious. He strokes his chin. He has a notebook open on his lap.

When the hymn is over, Mrs Hoolihan claps her hands.

"Ah yes!" she calls. "The Lord God indeed did make them all!"

She calms herself down. She raises her hands to calm all of us down.

"Now then, children," she says. "We have invited Mr Marsh and Miss Crystal back to our school for

one final time. They will explain everything. Make sure you listen closely."

She turns to Marsh.

"Over to you, Mr Marsh," she says. "Please give him your full attention, children!"

Eden Marsh stands up and we're all silent as the grave.

He tugs his shirt into place; he runs his fingers through his hair. He takes a deep breath. He pauses for a moment, then begins.

"Now, children," he says. "I haven't had the pleasure of meeting most of you yet. My name is Eden Marsh. My colleague here is Miss Crystal. And these two men are our helpers for today."

Miss Crystal smiles and waves. The burly blokes just nod.

"I realize," says Marsh, "that many of you might have been rather puzzled by what has been happening here this week. As well as being excited, of course. As well as being … entranced."

Another deep breath, another pause.

"Now it is time to shed some light. My colleagues and I are from an organization called New Life Corporation."

He shows us a logo bearing that name on the corner of the box.

"For some time now," he says, "with the support of the government and the educational authorities, we have been searching for a school in which to conduct one of the most important experiments of our time. We searched for a school that is neither truly outstanding nor miserably failing, a school led by teachers who are neither astonishing nor awful, containing children who are neither geniuses nor fools. We searched, in other words, for a school that is ordinary, led by ordinary teachers, inhabited by children who themselves are just ordinary. And after much research, we were led here, to Darwin Avenue Primary Academy, to your school, your ordinary little school."

Mrs Hoolihan is beaming, gasping, quivering.

"But before we move on," says Marsh. "I have been asked to give you a warning."

Another pause.

"I have been informed," he says, "that what we are about to demonstrate might be somewhat disturbing to children of a rather ... shall we say, nervous disposition. This is why we decided that the younger children should not be included."

He laughs. He shakes his head.

"For myself," he says, "I cannot imagine why what we are about to show you might have such an effect. But I must follow instructions, and I must warn you and ask you..."

He steps forward. He peers at us. He grins, as if the question he is about to ask is really silly, as if the answer is obvious.

"Is there anyone here," he says, "anyone here among you strong-looking, brave-looking, intelligent and modern young people, anyone whose disposition is ... *nervous?*"

No one speaks.

"Is there anyone," he asks, "who would like to *leave?*"

He grins again. He shrugs. He's turning away when Mrs Imani calls out, "Yes, Mr Marsh. There *are* children who are more nervous than others. I suspect that there *are* children who would like to leave."

"*Really?*" says Marsh.

"Yes," says Mrs Imani. "We who work with children day in and day out understand that some are more nervous than others, and that some children can find the challenges of life quite difficult."

Marsh rolls his eyes but says nothing.

Mrs Imani stands up.

"Children," she says, "there really is no need to stay if you would rather not."

Mrs Hoolihan stares at her but Mrs Imani ignores her.

"There's nothing wrong," she says, "with being nervous."

She smiles kindly. She calls some children by name, and soon a few children shyly stand up.

"Well done," says Mrs Imani. "That is very brave of you, children."

She looks at Eden Marsh.

"Don't you think they are brave, Mr Marsh?" she says.

He shrugs, says nothing.

"Why don't you children go to the library," says Mrs Imani.

"Thank you, Miss," they say, as they leave the hall.

We who are left gather closer.

"Ah well," Eden Marsh. "Maybe that shows that the warning was necessary."

He considers for a moment.

"But maybe it also shows," he says, "that it offered some children an *excuse*. And perhaps they will be very disappointed when they find out what they have missed."

Mrs Imani glares at him.

"Thank you, Mrs Imani," says Mrs Hoolihan. "Would anyone else like to leave? Excellent. On you go, Mr Marsh."

Marsh turns to the big blokes. He nods at them.

"And now," he says, "the box!"

They lift the box off the trolley. Then they slide away the trolley. They wheel away the trolley. They place the box beside the table. They go back to their seats.

Eden Marsh stands beside the box. It is slightly smaller than he is.

He takes a few deep breaths.

"We are here," he says, "to learn about George, the boy who has spent time with you, in your classrooms, in your yard and playing fields, in your streets, and even…" Here he seeks me out and smiles. "And even in your homes."

We are all very still. We are all very silent. Inside me, everything is seething.

There is a small handle on the right-hand side, halfway down the box. Marsh reaches across and grips that handle.

"I am about to show you," he says, "something that you will never forget. Are you ready?"

"Yes," say some in excitement.

"Yes," say some with a sense of dread.

No, I say inside myself. *Don't do it! Yes, you monster, do it now!*

Marsh smiles. He turns the handle, and pulls open the front of the box.

It's George. Of course it's George.

23

George. He is separated into parts: two arms, two legs, his body, his head. Each part rests in white polystyrene. His head faces out towards us. His eyes are closed.

There are gasps. There's screaming. A girl sitting beside me, Sanura Gupta, suddenly stands up with a cry. Mrs Imani reaches out to her. Kids get to their feet and follow the others to the library.

Marsh smiles.

"We knew, of course, that it would be something of a shock," he says. "But on the other hand, children, this is the truth. This is science. This is the making of history. This is a new world."

He pauses.

"And yes," he continues, "this really is our George."

He touches George's cheek.

"It is George, your friend. It is George, the boy who walked among you."

He strokes George's hair.

"And isn't he rather wonderful?" he says.

He waits for us to quieten.

"Now watch closely, children, and see the future taking shape."

He turns towards Miss Crystal.

"Miss Crystal," he says softly. "If you will."

She steps forward, all businesslike. She puts her black bag onto the table. She opens it and takes out some white gloves. She puts on the gloves.

"Don't worry, children," she tells us. "We'll show you all you need to know. Everything is well. There's nothing at all to be troubled about."

She reaches into the box and takes out George's left leg. She holds the leg before us then places it on the table.

Maxie curses.

Billy snarls.

Louise grits her teeth.

Miss Crystal continues. She takes out George's right leg and puts it on the table, then George's left arm and right arm. She lifts out George's body and lays it on the table. Only George's head remains in the box now, resting in its slot of polystyrene.

"Now, children," says Marsh. "Look very closely and Miss Crystal will recreate our George."

Miss Crystal smiles at us all again, then she takes out some tiny screwdrivers and tweezers from her bag. She begins to put together the body, the legs and the arms. We can see that there are clips and slots that need to be attached; there are cables and switches; there are thin coloured wires, tiny plugs and connectors.

"Look closely," says Marsh again. "See? It is all very simple."

And we do look closely. Even the ones who are horrified, even the ones who are crying, can't take their eyes away.

We see it all, how she makes the connections. We shuffle closer, lean closer. We hear the little clicks as switches snap into place. She twists the arms and legs into their slots on the body. They fit perfectly.

Miss Crystal slides George off the table so that he stands before us, headless.

Then, very gently, she reaches into the box and lifts out the head.

She pauses, then shows it to us. George's eyes

are closed. His face is very still.

I remember him calling me mate. I remember him stroking Ted and Koshka. I remember him saying no as Marsh got him into the van outside our house.

Is this really the same George?

"Oh, dear George!" calls someone.

We see that it's Mrs Imani. She has her own face in her hands.

"Oh, George!" she says again. "What have they done to you?"

Marsh grins and shakes his head, as if he's sorry for her, as if he thinks she's being silly. Then he nods at Miss Crystal.

Miss Crystal turns and places George's head onto George's shoulders. Again, there are connections to be made between the body and the head. Very slowly, very carefully, Miss Crystal makes these connections. She twists the head, presses, and *click*, it snaps into place. Then she takes a step back.

The reassembled George stands before us, dead still, eyes closed.

Eden Marsh stands with his hands on his hips watching Miss Crystal, watching us.

We are all very still.

Marsh nods at Miss Crystal again.

She reaches into her bag.

She takes out a remote control and shows it to us.

She points it towards George and presses a button.

George's eyes open.

She presses again.

George smiles.

"Hello, schoolmates," he says.

24

No one speaks.

There are squawks and gasps and cries, as if no one knows how to speak.

Marsh takes the remote control from Miss Crystal. He points and clicks.

George says it again.

"Hello, schoolmates."

"How are you, George?" says Marsh.

"I am perfectly splendid, thank you very much indeed."

George's mouth moves weakly as it always did. His eyes gaze out blankly as they always did.

"Thank you, George," says Marsh.

He stands at George's side. He is silent as he gazes at us. He has that oh-so-clever smile on his face.

He clicks and points again.

George bows to us.

"Do you understand now, children?" says Eden Marsh. "Do you see what our George is?"

"He's our mate," growls Maxie.

"He's our friend," says Louise.

"He's one of us," I say.

"This George," says Marsh, "*our* George, is very special. He is the first of his kind. And there will be others, a whole line of Georges, stretching into the future. We are so very proud of him," he adds, smoothing George's hair down.

"Leave him alone!" growls Louise.

Maxie stands up, then I do too.

Mr Sage glares, shakes his head at us. *Sit down!* he mouths.

Marsh spreads his hands.

"It's OK," he says. "I understand. I had mates myself, back when I was a lad. But you have to understand. George is not capable of being anybody's mate."

"Yes, he is!" says Maxie.

"No," says Marsh. "I'm sorry, but your … mate-ishness is simply a sign of how convincing our George is, of how well we have done our work. He is a *machine*, son."

"Don't call me son," Maxie mutters.

"Please sit down," says Marsh.

"Sit *down*, please," orders Mrs Hoolihan. "Let Mr Marsh explain."

Reluctantly we sit down.

"Thank you," says Marsh. "George is, of course, at a very experimental stage. He is the first walking, talking product of our New Life Corporation. We have been in the throes of creation for many years. We knew it was time to allow George to enter the world."

He smiles proudly.

"We have many competitors," he says. "Many rivals who would like to get their hands on George to understand how we have done it. But George is ours. We lead the way."

He puts his arm around George's shoulder, as if he is his best mate, as if George is his son.

"So what do you think?" says Marsh. "Did he seem real? Was he convincing? Did he seem just like you?"

There's a lot of whispering and chattering. Joyce Dunn from the year below us puts her hand up.

"Yes?" says Marsh.

"He did seem a bit like us, but as well he seemed like … dead weird or something."

"Dead weird?"

"Aye. Like he wasn't all there."

There's lots of sniggering.

"Aye," says somebody else. "Like you couldn't work out if he was really clever or really thick."

"I knew!" shouts Jack Frith.

"Knew what?" says Marsh.

"Knew he was a robot. I said to me sister when I went home. There's a new kid in school and he's a robot."

"I said he was an alien!" says somebody else. "He's come from Planet Zog, I said."

"Aye. I said the same and all. Stands to reason, I said."

"And," says Marsh, "did you *like* having him here? Did you enjoy your time with him?"

"Aye!"

"Yes!"

"It was a good laugh!"

"It's been dead interesting."

"That's excellent. So you felt that he fitted in, in his own … dead weird way."

"Aye, well, there's plenty weirdos here anyway!"

Marsh laughs. He leans towards us and lowers his voice as if he's sharing a great secret.

"One day, children," he says, "there will be a perfect George. A George will walk among you who is so perfectly made, so … human, that nobody will realize that it is a George at all. There will be a George – or a Georgina! – who seems to be just like you."

He watches us ponder that.

"So that *could* mean," says Sandra Miles, "that one of us here, right now, could be a … George, a robot, and we wouldn't know."

"Clever girl," says Marsh. "You are indeed correct." He looks at Mrs Hoolihan.

"What clever children you have in your school, Mrs Hoolihan!"

Mrs Hoolihan quivers with delight, of course.

"Oh, yes, we have, Mr Marsh!" she squeaks.

"Indeed, any single one of us," says Marsh, "might be a George, a robot."

"I'm not," mutters Billy.

"Maybe I am one myself!" says Marsh. "Maybe your head teacher is! Maybe the room is filled with creatures who *seem* to be human, but are not."

I look at Maxie.

"I'm not a robot, mate," he grunts.

"Me neither," I say.

"But I doubt it," says Marsh. "We at New Life Corporation are at the true cutting edge. No one else has come up with a way of creating the perfect-seeming human."

He steps back to George. He puts his arm around George's shoulder again.

"Our George is the star. Our George is a multimillion-pound project."

"*Multimillion-pound project*, children!" gasps Mrs Hoolihan.

"Yes," says Marsh. "And he is the first of a brand-new line."

"*A brand-new line!*"

Marsh cups George's chin in his hand. George, of course, makes no response. He gazes out at us all with empty eyes.

Mrs Imani speaks.

"Did *George* like it?" she says.

"Sorry?" says Marsh.

"Did he enjoy his time with us?" she says.

Marsh shrugs. He gives a little laugh.

"I'm not sure that's really the kind of question that can be answered."

"You could *ask* him, Mr Marsh."

Marsh shakes his head and grins. He points the remote at George, and clicks.

"George," he says, "did you enjoy your time in school with all these lovely children?"

George's mouth moves.

"I am perfectly splendid, thank you very much indeed," says George.

"So it seems that he did, Mrs…"

"Imani."

"Armani."

Mrs Imani glares at him. For a second, he glares back at her.

"But how did he *do* it?" someone calls.

"Do what?" says Marsh.

164

"The football!"

"The mental maths!"

"Ah, now we are getting to the heart of it," says Marsh. "Dear George and all of his great talents are simply the result of the most astonishing technological wizardry!" He pauses. "Shall we demonstrate?"

"Yes!"

Marsh smiles.

Miss Crystal steps forward with the black bag in her hand. She grins.

"We must begin, children," she says, "by removing George's ear."

25

George is motionless as Miss Crystal uses a tiny tool to take away his ear. She places the ear onto the table. Carefully, Marsh turns George so that the side of his head with the missing ear is facing us. Marsh beckons us forward. We shuffle even closer.

In the space left by the ear, we see that there are cables, plugs and connectors.

"You see them?" says Marsh.

"Yes."

"George is a very simple device in many ways," says Marsh. "He is a machine – like your own computer, like your TV, like your parents' cars – and like all machines, he needs power so that he can work. He needs to be *charged*."

He shows us a little connection point.

"Electrical power goes in there. We plugged him

into the mains this morning so he is fully charged and ready for anything. Do you recall seeing him fall on Monday? Yes? Simple. He just needed to be powered up again, which we did inside the van."

He points to another connection slot.

"But this," he says, "is where George becomes really interesting. This is where George becomes George."

He pauses and widens his eyes as if in wonder.

"This," he says, "is where we pour in all of George's skills and talents."

"Even *football?*"

"Yes, even football. *Everything.* Through that tiny slot behind George's ear. How astonishing, how *wonderful*, is that?"

He looks at us, lets that sink in.

"At present," he says, "George is almost empty. He has the basic ability, as you have seen, to walk and to talk a little. But we have taken away much that we had given him, such as that football, and that mental maths. Right now, George could not even tell you what 2 + 2 is."

"Why have you done that?" Mrs Imani again.

Marsh shrugs, as he does.

"George has no need of them, Mrs Imani. He

is part of an ongoing project. He is a stage in the development of—"

"Of what, Mr Marsh?"

"Of new forms of life, Mrs Imani."

He stares at her; she stares back at him. He turns to us again.

"We could put just about anything in here, children. The history of the Crusades. The ability to speak Russian. The laws of quantum physics. The ability to run a marathon in thirty minutes."

Billy groans loudly.

"Wish they could do that to me!"

Marsh hears him. He grins.

"I'm so pleased you said that, lad. For one day, maybe one day not too very far away, we *will* be able to do just that!"

"Put in maths?" says Billy.

"Yes, son, put in maths. Put in anything. Bypass all the problems and difficulties that some of us have with learning."

He laughs again. He points the remote at Billy. He clicks it.

"Have maths, young man!" he says.

Billy rolls his eyes and squeaks, as if great changes are happening inside him. He frowns then stares straight ahead just like George does.

"I am a mathematical genius!" he says. "Ask me anything!"

"What's 2 + 2?" I say.

"7!" replies Billy.

Marsh laughs.

"So here's the question," calls out Molecular Marx.

"Yes?" says Marsh.

"Would you say, Mr Marsh, that George is … intelligent?"

Marsh smiles.

"Ah. That is, of course, the crucial question. And it all depends on what we might mean by the word intelligence. George can do things. He can be *made* to do things. But does he *know* that he does these things? Can he … *think*?"

He stares at us all.

"What do you think, children?" he asks.

I look at George, standing there in front of us, with his empty eyes gazing at us. *Is* he thinking? Is he seeing us the way that we see him?

Some kids call yes. Some kids call no.

Someone yells out, "What do you think, George? Are you intelligent?"

No answer, of course.

Marsh shrugs.

"Maybe in the future we will create a being that is indeed capable of independent thought. But George is not that being. He is just a stage in the process."

"Just a *stage?*" says Louise.

"Yes, dear. George, for instance, does not even know that he is George."

"Yes, he does!" shouts someone.

Marsh turns to George. He points and clicks.

"Who are you, George?" he asks.

George blinks.

"I am perfectly splendid, thank you very much indeed," he says.

Marsh shrugs again.

"You are indeed," he says.

"So no," says Marsh to Marx and to us all. "I would not say that he is intelligent the way we all are. But we'll get there. And in the meantime … what shall we give to George today? What shall we have George *do?*"

"Do my homework!"

"Get rid of my big brother!"

"Make him dance!"

"Ah!" says Marsh. "Dance, eh? There's an idea. Miss Crystal, shall we show these children how beautifully our dear George can dance?"

Miss Crystal opens her bag. She takes out a little laptop and sets it on the table. She switches it on and leans forward, scrolling through reams of type. She points at something on the screen. Marsh looks; he nods.

"That will be perfect," he says.

Then Miss Crystal takes out a long cable. She attaches one end of the cable to the computer; she attaches the other end to a plug in the opening where George's ear had been. She taps some keys.

"We must wait just a few short moments," says Marsh.

After a few moment, Miss Crystal disconnects the cable from the computer and from George's head.

"Are we ready?" says Marsh.

Miss Crystal smiles and nods.

Marsh takes a deep breath.

He points the remote and clicks.

"George," he says. "Will you dance for us, please?"

George doesn't move.

171

"Children," says Marsh, "would you ask George to dance for us?"

"Go on, George!" call the voices.

"You can do it, George!"

"Dance, George! Dance!"

And George blinks, shudders, then spreads his arms wide, raises his head high, steps to the side, and starts to dance.

26

It's a kind of dance but it's like there's no rhythm or music to it. George steps stiffly from side to side. He spins slowly. He jumps a few inches and lands with a thud. He jumps again. He swings his arms and almost stumbles. He keeps going, tottering about in front of us. He lifts his feet and knees and bobs his head like a doll. His eyes are empty, like he sees nothing, hears nothing. He spins and sways and twirls and is clumsy and jagged and jerky.

Some of the kids chant his name. They clap and urge him on. Mrs Hoolihan claps too. I don't.

"Go on, George!" says Marsh. "Dance, George. Dance!"

He leans back and roars with laughter. He invites us to laugh along with him.

"Leave him alone," I say.

"Leave him alone," says Maxie.

"Leave him alone," says Billy Dodds.

Marsh doesn't hear. He pumps his fist in the air, then he points the remote again and clicks and George comes to a sudden halt.

He stands dead still, gazing out at us through his empty eyes.

"So," says Marsh, "as you see, our George can dance, though maybe not quite as well as some of you children can."

He holds up the remote.

"And as you also see, we can bring George to a stop with a single touch."

He smiles. He looks at the clock and then at Mrs Hoolihan.

"But our time is disappearing, I think, is it not?"

He beams at us.

"The holidays approach!"

Mrs Hoolihan says that yes they do, and she comes to his side.

"This is not the end," she says. "And in the days and weeks to come, we shall be writing and reflecting about our experiences in order to help with Mr Marsh's research."

"My colleagues and I are deeply grateful," says Marsh.

"We here at Darwin Avenue Primary Academy," says Mrs Hoolihan to us all, "are indeed at the cutting edge. Aren't we so lucky, children?"

"Yes! Yes!"

Louise raises her hand.

"Please, sir, Mr Marsh?" she says.

"Yes, young lady?"

"What will happen to George now?" she asks.

"Good question!" says Marsh. "Well, George will go back with us to our lab. We will try out a few more experiments on him." He laughs. "We will continue to protect him from the prying eyes of our rivals, of course! We will write up our research. But as I said, George is just a stage. He will lead to George Two, an upgraded model, a model that is closer to … to being just like you! And then there will be George Three and George—"

"So you'll abandon George?"

"I wouldn't say *abandon*, dear. He has never been intended to last for ever. Quite soon he will run out, break down, come to a final stop, just like a car does, or a washing machine."

"*Washing machine?*" says Louise.

"It could be," continues Marsh, "that we will use some of him for spare parts."

"*Spare parts,*" she echoes.

"Of course! We wouldn't want anything going to waste, would we? George is packed with very special components that can be used again. And after, the plan is that he will be displayed in a scientific museum."

"A *museum?*" she says.

"Yes. Isn't that wonderful, children? You will be able to visit him. And I'm sure that the work of the children of Darwin Avenue will be given full credit."

"We'll be famous!" someone calls.

"You will indeed," says Marsh.

He nods at Miss Crystal. She connects the cable to George and to the computer again. She presses keys. George stands there, allowing everything to happen.

"This is just the beginning," says Marsh. "Just think what it might all lead to, children."

He steps closer to us.

"One day," he says, "perhaps one day very soon, a boy – or indeed a girl! – created by the New Life Corporation, will walk among you, and you will believe that he was born just as you were and that he grew just like you did."

He pauses, to let his words sink in.

"But for now," he says, "this is the end of our George. Miss Crystal, please dismantle it."

Carefully, delicately, Miss Crystal undoes everything she did before. Undoes the connections, unclips the clips. Takes off the head and sets it back into the polystyrene. Takes off the arms, takes off the legs, sets them back into their slots. Lifts the body into its polystyrene slot.

And there is George, in pieces, dead still, dead silent, eyes closed, back in his box.

"Perhaps before I shut it in again," says Marsh, "you would like to say goodbye, children."

"Goodbye!" call some.

"Farewell, George!"

Marsh reaches for the handle.

"Any more final questions?" he asks.

"Yes!" calls Mrs Imani. "Do you love him, Mr Marsh?"

Marsh pauses and stares at her.

"*Love* him?" he says.

"Yes. Love him. I love my children. Do you love George?"

Marsh shrugs. He grins.

"I really don't think you understand, Mrs Armani. It is a *machine*. How could *love* have anything to do with a machine?"

They stare at each other.

Then Marsh pulls the handle, and the door closes, and George is shut inside. And the two big blokes step forward with their trolley and they put the box onto the trolley and they wheel it away.

And Marsh and Miss Crystal follow.

"We'll get him back," I say.

"But how?" says Louise.

"I don't know," I say. And I really don't know.

But we'll try.

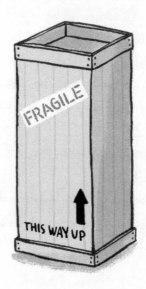

27

We all stand up when we're told to stand up.

We leave the hall when we're told to leave the hall.

We troop through the corridors when we're told to troop through the corridors.

We follow the teachers and head for the square classrooms.

"We're the robots," I say to Maxie.

"Aye, nowt but robots," grunts Billy Dodds.

We pass Mrs Hoolihan's office. They're all in there. George's box is standing in the corridor outside.

I lean close to the box. I imagine George in there, in the darkness.

"We'll get you back," I whisper.

But even as I whisper it, I know that it's impossible.

There's the black van in the yard outside, waiting to take him away. There's all the powerful adults.

Mrs Hoolihan comes back out into the corridor.

"No classrooms just yet," she says. She's quivering with delight. "There are photographs to take! Out you come, children. We'll do it in the sunshine at the front entrance."

So now we all troop outside. We stand where we're told to stand. We smile when we're told to smile. We keep changing where we stand, who we stand with. Marsh and Mrs Hoolihan and Miss Crystal and the two big blokes stand in the middle. We pose with the box, without the box; the box is rolled away to the van.

Some of us have to hold a banner saying **NEW LIFE CORPORATION – WHERE THE FUTURE IS CREATED.**

Others have to hold a brand-new school banner that Mrs Hoolihan unrolls with pride: **DARWIN AVENUE PRIMARY ACADEMY – AT THE CUTTING EDGE.**

We're told to smile, to clap, to wave our arms, to cheer.

"Had enough of this," groans Billy. "I'm off to me shed."

Mrs Hoolihan shouts after him but he takes no notice and she doesn't really care. She shrugs. After all, it's only Billy Dodds.

I can't stand it.

"Let's get out as well," I say to Maxie, but then Marsh points and asks especially for me.

"Yes, you, lad!" he says. "You're the boy who took George home, aren't you?"

I don't move.

"Don't be shy, son!" he says. "You're a great kid, lad!"

The burly blokes come and usher me to Marsh's side. I have to stand with his big strong stupid arm around my shoulder. I have to shake his big strong stupid hand.

"I hope you're proud," he whispers in my ear. I can smell the deodorant on him.

I want to tell him I'm not; I want to tell him I can't stand him.

Marsh shakes Mrs Hoolihan's hand for the last time. He punches the air. He makes his way through us all. He stops to sign autographs as he goes.

"Enough! Enough!" he says, like he can't bear the adulation.

He tells us we're lovely; we're beautiful; we're great kids; he'll never forget us.

The blokes load George's box into the van, and they all climb in. They drive away. The van's horn hoots as they slide out through the gates. The gates slide shut behind them. Kids continue cheering.

Louise is at my side.

"He's gone," she sighs.

"He's gone," I say.

"Gone," says Maxie.

Then Billy's suddenly standing with us.

"I've got him," he whispers.

"What?"

"George. He's in me shed."

28

"Quick!" says Billy. "They'll be back for him soon as they find out. We got to get him out."

We don't know how to speak. We don't know how to move. We don't know what to do.

"Bring your bags," says Billy. "Now, when everybody's leaving."

We still don't move.

"Now!" says Billy.

We hurry back to the classroom. Mr Sage is still full of the wonder of what we've seen.

"Well?" he says. "Was I right or was I wrong? Was it something you'll never forget?"

I can't think. I can't answer.

"Come *on!*" he says. "You've never seen anything like that before, have you?"

"No," I blurt out.

"No," says Maxie.

"No," says Louise.

He laughs.

"Look at you all," he says. "Listen to you all. Totally flabbergasted. Totally *discombobulated*! What a treat!"

"We're off now, Mr Sage," I say.

"Have a good holiday, Mr Sage," says Maxie.

"I will indeed, Maximilian."

We stumble out of the classroom. We try to stroll across the yard like nothing's up, twisting our way through the kids.

"Where're you lot going?" yells Nintendo Norah.

"Just getting Billy, Miss!" I yell back.

"Well, get a move on. It's not every week I have an extra hour on a Friday night."

We reach Billy's shed. He's waiting just inside.

"We take a bit each," he says.

I can hardly breathe. There he is, George, in pieces, resting on Billy's seed trays.

"Do it!" says Billy. "Take a bit each and get him out. Daniel. The head!"

"The head?"

"Aye. Get it into the drum box, man."

"*What?*"

Then I understand. I take my drum out of its

box and put it into the back of Billy's cupboard. I lift up George's head – *I lift up George's head!* – and I put it in the drum box. Maxie gets George's legs and puts them in his sports bag. Louise gets George's arms and puts them in her violin case. And Billy gets George's body and puts it in his garden sack.

And then we head back outside. We still try to stroll; we still try to make out this is all just ordinary. There's still lots of kids streaming out through the gates. My heart is pounding; my brain is boiling.

"Daniel?" somebody says.

I jump. It's Mrs Imani. She's just getting into her car.

"Is everything all right, Daniel?" she asks.

"Aye, Miss. Aye."

She frowns. She peers at us.

"Are you *all* all right?"

"Aye, Miss," I say.

"Please, Miss," says Louise. "We've got to go, Miss. *Please.*"

Mrs Imani gasps and bites her lip. Her eyes widen. We hold our breath.

"Go on," she tells us. "Run like the wind. Have a good holiday, children."

And we leave, and hurry through the gates past Nintendo Norah. We run like the wind into our estate, and pause for a brief moment under the flowering cherry tree. And we stand in a circle there and stare in fright and wonder at one another.

"What'll we do?" whispers Louise.

"Hide him," says Billy.

"Keep him safe," I say. "Keep him secret."

"Just act normal," says Maxie. "They'll never think it's us."

"There'll be a time to put him back together," says Louise.

"And make him into George again," I say.

"Now run," says Billy. "Get him home. Get him hid."

And so we separate, and we run again, and we get him hid.

29

Mam gets home late that day. Her bright blue *The New You* van pulls up outside the house and in she comes, full of smiles. Dolly Hanlan from Baudelaire Street's getting married tomorrow, and Mam's been run off her feet all day doing nails and hair.

"And in the middle of it all, what does Dolly herself want but the full double leg wax!"

She laughs.

"But I don't suppose you want to know about Dolly's double leg wax, do you?"

"No, Mam."

"Or about her screaming."

"No, Mam."

She grins and tousles my hair.

"It's getting long again," she says. "We'll trim it tomorrow, eh?"

"Aye, Mam."

"There was a lad come in last week to get his hair dyed blue," she says. "It looked very nice. Do you fancy that, Dan?"

"No, Mam."

"It'd suit you. It'd go with your eyes."

She giggles, yawns, stretches.

"I'm jiggered and starving," she says. "How about a Friday night pizza?"

"Aye, Mam."

Then she frowns.

"Is everything all right, Dan?"

"Aye, Mam."

A car drives past outside. I flinch, and look at the window.

"Are you sure?" she says.

"Aye, Mam."

She keeps on peering at me.

"What's going on?" she says.

"Nothing, Mam."

"Daniel, what's going on?"

I sigh. How does she always know?

"It's George," I say.

"George? Your new mate?"

"Aye."

"What about him?"

I don't even know how to start.

"Did you think he was," I say, "a bit … weird?"

"Weird? Yes, I suppose so. But you kids are all a bit weird if you ask me. And to tell the truth, it'd be weird if you weren't."

She laughs at that.

"He was canny enough, wasn't he?" she says. "No bother, very polite. And didn't our Koshka just love him!"

"He's a robot," I say.

"He's a *what*?"

"A robot. Or something like a robot. Or at least he was till they took him apart."

She doesn't say anything to that. She just stares at me. She stares at the ceiling.

"I'll tell you what," she says. "I'll pour meself a

191

glass of wine and you can tell me it again."

She pours the wine. I keep watching the window. I keep expecting the black van to turn up outside.

"So we had a robot here for tea?" she says. "Or something like a robot? And now he's in pieces?"

"Aye, Mam."

"Tell me again," she says, "and I'll see if it makes sense this time."

"George," I say, "is a robot. He—"

"No. Tell it right from the start."

So I explain about George turning up at school, and about the maths and the football and about Eden Marsh.

"The bloke that came with the van?"

"Aye, Mam."

"Now him, he was definitely a weird one. Go on, son."

So I go on, right up to when Miss Crystal took George apart and put him back in his box.

Mam stares at the wall.

"Am I expected to believe this?" she says.

"I saw it all, Mam. We all saw it all. And you saw George, didn't you?"

"This isn't something that you and Maxie dreamed up?"

"No, Mam."

"So where is George now?"

I bite my lip. I can feel my heart thudding. There's no way I can tell her the truth.

"I don't know, Mam." My hands are trembling. "He's back at the lab, I suppose, Mam. Or…"

Suddenly the phone's ringing. Mam picks it up.

"It's *Mrs Hoolihan*," she whispers.

She frowns.

"She wants a word." She passes the phone to me.

"H-hello, Mrs Hoolihan." I try to stop my voice from wobbling but it's hers that's the wobbly one.

"Daniel," she gasps. "Something *terrible* has happened."

193

"Has it, Miss?"

"I'm not even supposed to talk about it. It's *top secret*."

"Is it, Miss?"

"Yes. But you're his friend, aren't you? *Weren't* you?"

"Whose friend, Miss?"

"His. George's."

"Yes, Miss. Are you OK, Miss?"

"You haven't seen him, have you?"

"Seen *who*, Miss?"

She lowers her voice.

"*George!*" she whispers.

"George?" My hands are sweating. "No, Mrs Hoolihan. He's in his box, isn't he? They took him away, Miss, didn't they?"

"Course you haven't. Course he is. Course they did. Forget I even asked!"

"OK, Miss."

"It was the rivals," says Mrs Hoolihan. "Of course, it must have been the rivals, like they said it was. But what a thing to

194

happen at Darwin Avenue Primary Academy."

"For what to happen, Mrs Hoolihan?"

"Nothing, Daniel. Forget I ever phoned."

Mam reaches for the phone again.

"Are you OK, Mrs Hoolihan?" she asks.

I lean close and hear Mrs Hoolihan squeaking that yes, she's absolutely fine, thank you very much indeed.

"And is it really true that George was a…"

"Yes. Yes! He was a…"

Mam smiles softly and goes all gentle.

"Take it easy, Mrs Hoolihan. It's not every week you have a robot in your school, is it?"

"No," squeaks Mrs Hoolihan.

"Exactly. It must be very hard to cope with. Bad enough having the ordinary kids to deal with, isn't it?"

"Yes," says Mrs Hoolihan. "And I'll never have any robots in school ever again."

"That's good," says Mam. "Now, tell you what. Why don't you drop into the salon sometime and I'll give you a nice head massage. That'd help to calm you down, wouldn't it?"

"Yes," squeaks Mrs Hoolihan. "I'll do that. Do you do waxing as well?"

"We do indeed. It'd do you the world of good. So why not pop in soon and I'll give you the head to toe at a knock-down rate."

"Yes. Oh, thank you, yes!"

"You'll be a new you, Mrs Hoolihan."

"Will I?"

"Yes. Now forget about all this and have yourself a nice holiday."

"Thank you. Oh, thank you very much indeed."

Mam puts the phone down.

"Poor Mrs Hoolihan," she says.

She shakes her head.

"So it's all true?"

"Yes, Mam."

"Poor soul. It's hard enough being a head teacher without having to cope with robots as well."

A vehicle drives past, doesn't stop.

"I'll give her the full treatment," says Mam. "Seaweed body wrap, the works."

"Good idea, Mam," I say. My heart has stopped thudding now.

Then she leans forward suddenly and stares into my eyes.

"*You're* not a robot, are you?"

I put on a mechanical-sounding voice.

"Me am robot boy," I say. "Me am made of metal. Me am not your son."

"Ah well, that clears that up. Now let's get those pizzas on, eh? Do you eat pizza, Robot Boy?"

"Yes. Robot Boy in love with pizza."

She goes to the fridge. She pauses and ponders.

"A little drop of olive oil," she says. "And a bit of dead dry cake. All that 'I am perfectly splendid, thank you very much indeed.' Now it all makes sense."

"Does it?" I say.

She laughs.

"Kind of."

"I've got to go to the loo," I tell her.

I run upstairs and slip into my bedroom. I'm scared to look inside the wardrobe but I make myself open the door a few inches. I reach in and lift up a pile of underpants and T-shirts.

There he is. There *it* is, George's head, dead still, eyes closed, resting on the shelf, all alone in the dark.

"George," I whisper.

Of course there's no response.

I cover the head again, and shut the door. I go to the window and look out at the estate, at the kids playing happily on the grass.

One sees me and waves. It's one of the fairy lasses from Reception.

I wave back. I want to yell at her, "Come and see the multimillion-pound robot head in my wardrobe!"

But I don't.

The smell of cooking pizza comes from down below.

"Do you want olives on it?" yells Mam.

"A-aye, Mam!"

I feel Koshka nuzzling against my leg.

"Hello, Kosh," I say.

Koshka purrs, then scratches at the wardrobe door, like he knows.

"Your mate's back," I whisper.

Then I'm shivering, in excitement, in dread.

30

It's a weird evening. How could it not be a weird evening? I keep listening out for the van, looking at the window. The pizza's delicious. Mam's tired. She'll have another long and busy day tomorrow doing hair and nails and skin. Business is booming. I tell her it's because she's brilliant. She smiles at that. She says she loves having her own salon, but she needs more staff to help her keep up. It's so hard to find the right people.

She laughs.

"Mebbe sometime soon," she says, "there'll be robots that can work in beauty salons."

"Mebbe," I say.

"But that's unlikely, isn't it? You've got to be really caring if you're going to make people feel nice about themselves. You've got to be really kind to give people makeovers that'll change their lives."

She ponders a few moments while she sips her wine.

"Maybe robots *could* be kind and caring," she says. "Maybe they *could* give gentle massages and file people's nails with love. Do you think so, Dan?"

I think about Eden Marsh. Do people like him *want* to make robots that are kind and caring? Could robots themselves just turn out to be kind and caring? Or would robots made by people *like* Eden Marsh turn out to be robots like Eden Marsh?

"I dunno, Mam," I say.

"George looked like he could be kind," she says. "Was he kind?"

I wonder about that. He *was*, sort of.

"Don't really know," I say. "He wasn't really around long enough for us to find out, Mam."

"Poor George. Needed a bit more time with us all, didn't he?"

"Aye, Mam."

"A bit more time with ordinary folk."

"Aye, Mam."

"So strange," she says, "to think he came into the world without a mam and dad. And grew up in the world with nobody caring for him and cuddling him."

She pauses, like she's amazed by her thought.

"And he was never even born. How can something be alive if it wasn't even born?"

We're both still and silent as we think about it. She leans right across to me and holds me tight and tells me that she loves me, that she's always loved me.

"I know that, Mam," I whisper.

She lets go.

"Pity they took him apart again," she says. "I could've cuddled him as well."

"Aye, Mam. Aye."

I think about George's head upstairs.

I try not to think about George's head upstairs.

She picks up the remote.

"Fancy some telly?" she says.

"Aye."

There's a rerun of *Doctor Who* on. The Cybermen are stamping down a dark steel corridor while somebody yells and screams in horror. I remember how the Cybermen used to terrify me just a couple of short years ago, how they gave me nightmares. And they suddenly terrify me again now.

Mam laughs. She remembers too.

I click the remote and the Cybermen disappear.

I click it again and back they come.

I click it again and off they go.

"Make your mind up," says Mam.

"Sorry."

"Mebbe it was just as well George went back into his box," says Mam.

She tries to laugh.

"We've got to be careful what we unleash into the world."

"Aye, Mam."

We're quiet for a while. She reads her book. I try to read as well: *The Graveyard Book*. It's brilliant, but I can't concentrate. My mind keeps drifting back to George, to the wardrobe upstairs.

I keep glancing at the remote in my hand.

I feel Mam looking at me.

"I could get the scissors and do it now," she says.

"What?"

"Your hair."

"Oh. No. It's OK, Mam. Think I'll go up to me room."

"OK, son."

I drop the remote and get up.

"Look out for the Cybermen," she says as I shut the door.

I go upstairs. I look out the window. It's getting dark outside. There's Mam's bright blue van. All the little kids have gone in. There's the sound of a siren far away. There's a pale half-moon hanging over the rooftops. I think of George, the different parts of him scattered across the estate.

Something shifts in the room behind me. I turn fast, but it's only Koshka coming in.

I phone Maxie.

"What we gonna do?" I whisper.

He can't talk long. The vicar's there.

"Keep it quiet," he whispers. "Keep him hid."

"Aye," I say. "Aye." I pause. "I'm a bit scared, Maxie."

"Me as well. But there's no way they can know it's us."

"No."

"We'll need power," he says. "We'll need a cable so we can do it."

"*It?*"

"*It.* You know what I mean, Dan."

"Where'll we do it, though? When?"

"Dunno. We'll sort it out. Keep it quiet. Keep him hid. I've got to go."

He goes. I hear my mam running a bath. She shouts that she'll be having an early night. Busy day tomorrow.

"OK, Mam."

I listen to her moving about. I sit on the bed with Koshka on my lap.

I hear her go into the bathroom and I hear her step into the bath. She shouts to tell me that the water is delicious. I lie for ages while the darkness deepens outside. Then she's out of the bath again. She knocks on my door and comes into my room with her dressing gown on.

"OK, son?" she says.

"Aye, Mam."

"Good lad."

She tousles my hair and kisses me on the brow.

"I'm very glad you're not a robot," she says.

"Me, too."

"Night-night, son."

"Night-night, Mam."

"Sleep," she sighs. "Delicious lovely sleep."

And she leaves me. I hear her going into her room, closing the door behind her.

I wait for a few moments. I take a deep breath and open the wardrobe door and lift out George's head.

31

I sit on the bed. I hold the head in my hands. I rest it on my lap, then put my hands around my own head to feel how big it is. A bit bigger than George's. I think about all the things that are going on in there. My head's filled with memories. All the stories I've heard, all the people I've met, all the telly I've seen, all the books I've read, all the places I've been. It's haunted by dreams: Cybermen and wolves, fairies and starships. It's filled with hopes and troubles and fears. It can think about mental maths and Vasco da Gama. It can imagine Australia and pizza and prawn cocktail crisps and cherry trees and Mars. It can think about my mates and feel happy. It can think about people like Eden Marsh and feel angry.

What about George's head? I hold it again. It's about as heavy as a football. The skin feels like human skin. The hair feels like human hair. The cheeks are nearly as soft as my own. I look at the closed eyes. Is anything going on in there, or is there really just nothing till something's put into it?

"George," I whisper, but of course there's no answer.

Koshka's stretched out beside us. He's purring. I lift the head high and look up into the neck. A few thin cables are there, tidied away into slots.

I hear Mam laughing and laughing again, and I know she's just having one of her barmy dreams.

I shudder suddenly at the thought of what I'm doing. I take a deep breath.

I inspect George's left ear. When I look closely I can see where it joins to George's head. I hold it gently and try to turn it, but nothing happens. I turn it the other way, but nothing. I tug. Nothing. There are a few coins on my bedside table. I get a twenty pence piece and try to slip it into the crack where the ear joins the head. I press. Nothing. I try a five pence piece. Nothing. I twist. Nothing. I'm about to give up and look for a screwdriver or something, when suddenly it works. The ear drops away from the head. Koshka reaches out a paw for it but I pick it up and put it under the pillow.

Then I look again, at where the ear was.

There's the little row of connection points that we saw in school. They're like the points at the side of a computer. There's a power point, and a couple of ordinary USB points.

"Don't touch," I say to Koshka.

I put the head on the pillow but realize Koshka won't be able to help himself, so I hold the head under my arm as I get off the bed to find my laptop charger.

I catch sight of myself in the mirror. I stop and stand in front of it and look at myself with George's head tucked under my arm. So weird. I lift it and rest it on my shoulder. I'm the boy with two heads.

I find the charger and plug it in but don't switch it on yet. I touch the other end of the charger cable to the connection in George's head.

It clicks into place.

It fits.

I look at the dark outside. I look at the moon. I hear Mam. This time she's snoring, then she stops and everything goes very quiet and very still.

I lean down and switch the charger on at the wall.

Nothing happens. I'm about to switch it off

again. Then I feel it, just a tiny vibration in George's head. There's a very low humming sound. I think I feel the head becoming warm. I think the eyes are about to open.

I lean down and switch it off. I detach the cable and wrap it up again. I put the ear back on. I put the head back into the wardrobe.

I tell myself not to scream.

I text Maxie.

We can do it. We can make George live.

Course we can, he answers.

I sit on the bed with Koshka on my lap, looking out into the dark.

An aeroplane drones over the estate.

I text Maxie again.

We'll do it tomorrow.

They'll be looking for him.

Not here. They think it's the rivals.

Do they?

Yes.

Are you sure?

Aye.

Where'll we do it?

My place. My mam'll be out all day.

OK. What time?

Ten. I'll text the others.

OK.

There's a long pause.

I'm scared, he texts.

Me too.

I text Billy and Louise. I tell them they think it's the rivals. I tell them we'll do it here at ten.

OK, texts Billy.

OK, texts Louise.

I text Maxie again.

It's on. Ten, my place. We'll make him live.

Aye. We'll make him live!

A bit later, I text them all again.

Bring a remote.

OK.

OK.

OK.

I clean my teeth and get into bed. Koshka's on the covers beside me, purring. I can't get to sleep. When I do drift off, I dream about Cybermen stamping up the stairs. I dream about Mrs Hoolihan wrapped in seaweed. Then I dream that Marsh and Miss Crystal come into my room; Miss Crystal has the black bag in her hand. Marsh nods.

"Get on with it, Miss Crystal," he says.

Miss Crystal opens the bag and takes out some instruments. She takes off my head and throws it out of the window and it lands in the branches of the cherry tree. I see my body leaning against the tree trunk below; I see my legs running around all by themselves. My arms are walking on their hands like in *The Addams Family*. The fairy lasses are dancing and laughing around them on the green.

"Good morning, Robot Boy," says Mam.

I open my eyes and there she is at the bedroom door.

"I've got to go," she says. "Maxie'll be coming round, will he?"

"Aye, Mam. We'll be fine, Mam."

"That's great."

Soon I hear her van starting up and driving away.

Koshka's scratching at the wardrobe.

I don't open it.

32

I sit at the kitchen table. The sun's streaming in through the window. I drink tea and eat toast and marmalade. Kids are already out playing in the streets. Koshka's out there too, wandering about like he does. I tell myself this is still the dream world. I haven't got the head of a robot in my wardrobe. My mates aren't coming round with remote controls and the robot's other body parts. There are no such people as Eden Marsh and Miss Crystal.

I shake my head and laugh at the whole idea of it. I'll wake up soon, go across to Maxie's and we'll play computer games or football or lumber through the streets like zombies, frightening the little kids.

There's a movement outside and I see Louise coming towards the kitchen door. She's got the violin case in her hand. I let her in.

"I'm the first?" she says.

"Aye."

"And you're sure it's safe to get on with it today?"

"Aye."

She opens the case and puts George's arms on the table beside the teapot and the jar of marmalade. We just look at them.

"I couldn't sleep," she says.

"Me neither."

Then Maxie and Billy are here together, carrying their bags.

Everybody's trembling, everybody wants to forget all about it and everybody can't wait until we start.

"Do it in here?" says Billy.

"No," I say. "Upstairs. Just in case anybody comes." I lock the kitchen door. Up we go to my bedroom.

Louise carries the arms. Billy and Maxie take the legs and the body out of their bags.

We lay the legs, the body and the arms on the bed. I get the head out and put it in place.

Maxie starts giggling.

"We're making a robot!" he snorts. He can hardly get his words out.

"Anybody got the instructions?" says Billy.

Then we're all snorting and giggling like little kids.

Eventually we calm down. We work out which is the left leg and which is the right, which is the left arm and which the right. Louise starts looking into the left armpit. She teases some wires out of the top of the arm. She sees where the connections are and clicks the wires into place. Then she twists the arm into the armpit and it snaps into place. She does the right arm in the same way.

Billy and Maxie do a leg each, connecting the wires, twisting the leg until it snaps into place.

I take the head. I tease out the wires from the neck and connect them to the ones coming from the opening to the body. They click easily into place. I push the head down but it doesn't fit properly. I try again. I hold it in both hands, push and twist and – *click!* – it's there.

We stand back and look down on him.

We can hardly breathe.

We can hardly look at one another.

"What now?" whispers Maxie.

I get the five pence piece and show them how to get the ear off and expose the connection points.

I show them how the computer charger clicks into the slot in George's head. I push the three pin plug into the socket on the wall.

"What if he does something terrible?" says Louise.

"He won't, will he?" says Billy.

"We don't know that."

We stand dead still. We don't know anything.

"What if he turns out to be a monster?" I say.

Nobody knows how to answer that.

"Only one way to find out," says Maxie.

He leans down to the socket and switches it on.

33

We all step back. We watch. We can't speak.

Then I hear it again, that low humming noise.

"Listen," I whisper.

We lean over the bed.

"Hell's teeth," says Maxie.

He reaches down and touches George's chest.

"Something's happening," he says.

We wait.

"How long will it take?" says Billy.

No answer.

George just lies there, dead still, eyes closed.

"Mebbe he's like a computer," says Louise. "He doesn't need to be fully charged before he starts to work."

"Did you bring the remotes?" I whisper. I get mine and point it at George. My hand's trembling. I click. I click again.

Nothing.

"He'll need something special," says Maxie. "We should have found a way to nick their remote as well."

Billy pulls a remote out of his pocket, points and clicks, points and clicks.

"As much use as a chocolate teaspoon," he says.

Louise fumbles in her violin case and gets out her remote.

"It's one of those multi-purpose ones. It cost a bomb. You can use it for lots of different things – tellies, computers, CD players."

She points and clicks. Nothing happens. She shrugs.

"But not for robots, apparently," she says.

Maxie tries one that he's brought along and nothing happens.

"Give it time," I say.

Billy laughs.

"We'll have a charged-up robot that just lies about in bed all day."

"Like me Uncle Joe," says Maxie.

Suddenly it all seems just stupid, not exciting or scary at all.

"What's the point of saving him if we can't get

him to work?" says Maxie. "That's not really saving him, is it?"

"They were going to use him for *spare parts*," says Louise. "And put him in a *museum*. We're saving him from all that."

"Aye, and that Marsh was a pain, wasn't he?" says Maxie.

We all agree.

"We could go to jail," I say.

"But it's not like stealing a *thing*," says Louise. "Is it? It's like stealing a person. Or nearly a person."

"Kidnapping," I say.

That makes us all pause.

"That's a proper crime," I say. "You get years for that."

"We'll blame Billy," says Maxie. "He was the one that done the deed."

"They were so stupid," Billy says. "So bothered about getting photos of themselves. I just had to open the box and get George out and into me shed. Quick and easy. They saw nowt."

"And we're doing it for *George*," says Louise. "Aren't we? You can't just make something live then switch it off again like it means nothing. Can you?"

"No," I say. "That's like murder."

"Aye!" says Billy. "Murder! They're the ones who should be in jail."

"And," I say, "we're doing it so he can…"

"So he can live again," says Maxie.

"Aye," says Billy. "So he can be … real. So he can be like us."

He leans down and pats George's head.

"Howay, George," he says. "Howay, mate. You can do it."

We all lean over George like we're trying to pour our energy and life into him.

"Come on," we whisper.

"Howay, George."

"You can do it, George."

"Don't worry, George," I whisper. "We're here. We'll look after you."

"Please," says Billy. "We'll be your mates."

"You'll have a great time," says Maxie.

And I have a vision of George running around with us in the estate. I see him sitting with us under the cherry tree. I see him smiling and I hear him laughing. And maybe we all get the same vision. Maybe we're all seeing George as he could be, as we want him to be, as we lean over him in my little bedroom with the sun shining down outside and slanting in through the window.

"*Come on, George.*"

"*You can do it, George.*"

"*You're great, George.*"

"*We…*"

We all pause. We take a deep breath.

"*We love you, George.*"

We laugh together when we've said that.

Then Louise gets her multi-purpose remote again.

And she clicks.

And George opens his eyes.

34

"Hello, schoolmates," George says. His voice is frail, like it comes from a thousand miles away. He doesn't move.

We all kneel by the bed.

"Hello, George," says Louise.

His eyes turn to her.

"We're your friends," she says. "Look. This is Daniel, and Billy and Maxie. I'm Louise."

"Do you remember us?" says Billy.

George doesn't answer.

"Are you OK?" I ask.

His tiny, distant voice again. The words come out of him so slowly.

"I am perfectly splendid, thank you very much indeed."

"You're in my bedroom," I tell him. "You came here before. You met Ted and Koshka."

I reach under the bed and find Ted. I put him on George's chest.

"Remember?" I whisper.

He says nothing. He stares up at the ceiling.

I hear Koshka scratching at the bedroom door as if he's been called. I let him in. Straight away, he jumps up onto the bed. He lies on George's arm and starts to purr. George doesn't move.

"You'll be OK, George," I whisper. "We'll make sure you're OK."

He does nothing, says nothing. I find myself thinking we shouldn't be doing this. It's all too hard for him. Maybe he doesn't want to come back to life again. Maybe he wants to stay in a box, or be taken apart for spare parts, or be put in a museum. Maybe he doesn't want anything, isn't capable of wanting anything. Maybe we're wrong. Maybe we're cruel.

What I do know is that we all want the best for George, whatever it turns out to be. And whatever it is that we're doing, we have to try to do it right.

"We should get him to sit up," says Maxie.

"Should we?" says Billy.

"Aye," says Maxie. "He's gonna have to move at some point, isn't he?"

So Maxie and I slide our hands under his shoulders and try to lift him.

"Come on, mate," I say. "Try and sit up."

He lets us lift him up and slide him back so that he's leaning against the wall. He's heavy, as heavy as any of us.

We let him sit there. We let him do nothing. Power from the cable continues to pour into him. Minutes pass and minutes pass. The sun moves over the estate. It's already afternoon.

"Can we get you anything?" says Louise.

George doesn't answer.

"Mebbe we need to put something into him," says Maxie. "Like they did with maths and football."

We all sigh. How can we do that?

Louise sings to him.

"All things bright and beautiful,
All creatures great and small.

"It's the song we sang in assembly, George," she says. "Remember?"

George closes his eyes, like he's disappeared again, or like he's listening.

"All things wise and wonderful,
The Lord God made them all."

Billy says he's starving, so I go down to get some biscuits and cheese and some Coke and stuff. When I come back up I can't believe it.

George is kind of singing, along with Louise, in his tiny, distant voice. Not the words, not the proper tune, just a kind of sweet groan, a kind of echo of Louise's voice.

We all listen. We're entranced. Then he stops.

"See," says Billy. "We *can* do it. We can put everything he needs into him."

"George," I whisper. "You're coming back, George."

He opens his eyes.

"Daniel," he says. "Billy. Louise. Maxie."

"That's right," says Maxie.

"Mates," says George, in his tiny voice. "Mates."

Then he closes his eyes again.

35

We let him rest. We let the power seep into him. We sit around eating biscuits and cheese and drinking Coke. The day passes by. George just slumps there, like he's exhausted. I wonder again if we should be doing this. I wonder again if we're cruel.

Billy thinks the same.

"Mebbe he doesn't want this," he says.

We know he might be right.

"Mebbe we've done enough for today," says Louise.

"Aye," I say. "Anyway, my mam'll be coming back. We'll have to hide him again."

"Where?" says Billy.

"We can't take him out. He'll have to hide in here, with me."

We look around my little room. In the wardrobe, of course.

We get George to move again. Maxie and I put our hands under his armpits and try to help him up. I feel how warm he's become, as warm as us.

"Come on, George," I say. "Try and stand up."

We turn him and he edges his feet over the side of the bed. I detach the charging cable from his head so he doesn't get tangled up in it. I click his ear back into place. We lift and he leans forward and stands. He totters for a moment, then gets his balance.

"Well done, George," says Louise.

"You're doing great," says Billy.

I realize he's standing in front of the window. I lean past him to pull the curtains shut. There's lots of kids out there, but nobody's looking up. Nobody will have seen.

"Open the wardrobe door, Billy," I say.

He does that.

We edge George forward. He puts one foot in front of the other.

"In here," I whisper. "Don't worry; you'll be OK."

We guide him into the wardrobe. I push a coat aside so he can stand up. We turn him so he's facing us. He gazes out through the shadows.

"Are you OK?" says Louise.

"I am perfectly splendid, thank you very much indeed," he answers.

We all lean forward to pat him on the shoulders and give him smiles of encouragement. We tell him that everything will be fine.

"Billy," he says. "Maxie. Daniel. Louise."

"That's right," says Louise. "That's great, George."

Koshka slips past us into the wardrobe. He sits at George's feet.

"Koshka," I say.

"Kosh-ka," says George softly.

Koshka purrs.

"Time to turn him off," says Maxie.

We catch our breath. We grit our teeth. He's right.

Louise fetches the multi-purpose remote.

"We'll come back for you, George," she says.

She points and clicks.

George's eyes close.

He stands there, dead still.

Louise puts the remote on a shelf in the wardrobe.

"It's always getting lost at home," she says. "They'll think it's down the side of the sofa or something."

I lift Koshka out.

"Poor George," says Louise. "He's been in a lab and a van and a box and a box again and a bag and another bag and a violin case and a wardrobe."

"One day you'll be free," says Billy.

"Aye," we all agree. "One day, George, you will be free."

We shut the door.

36

We say we'll get together again on Monday, when my mam will be at work again. It's hard to leave one another. We're more than a team, more than a bunch of mates. We've gone through something extraordinary today. We get our stuff together and go downstairs. We pause in the kitchen. Everything seems somehow different, even my ordinary old kitchen. The whole world, even the staircase, even the kitchen, is so different. *We're* so different. We look at one another, dazed, but we don't know how to say those things. We have a quick, awkward hug, the four of us, then let go.

I unlock the back door. We say goodbye. My friends step out into the afternoon spring light. I watch them as they leave the garden, leave each other, make their separate ways through the streets of the transformed estate towards their own homes.

I watch until they're gone. I keep looking at the pale houses, the bright green grass, the trees, the children playing, birds flying, the cars glinting in the sun. Then I close the door again. I don't know what to do. I want to sing or pray or cry or laugh, so I do all those things, then I find myself doing some weird dance, as if there's something in me making me do it, something that comes from deep, deep down inside, that makes my body sway, makes my legs and arms swing, makes me close my eyes and stretch downwards to the earth and upwards to the sky.

Then I laugh at myself. I laugh and laugh and laugh.

Then here's Mam's van pulling up outside and here's Mam coming in through the door.

I'm still laughing. She grins.

"Had a good day with Maxie, son?"

"Aye, Mam. You had a good day, Mam?"

"Aye, son." She starts laughing too.

"What's the joke?" I say.

"Everything!" she says. "That Mrs Benson and her funny feet. Lewie Patel and her rainbow hair.

231

The tattoo on Betty Ainsworth's bum. That Mrs Hoolihan!"

"Mrs Hoolihan?"

"Aye. She popped in to make her appointment. Asked if we did head transplants cos she wanted to get the worries out of her brain."

She laughs and laughs.

"And you," she says.

"Me?"

She cups my chin in her hand and kisses me.

"Aye, you," she says. "You're such a weird one."

"I know that, Mam, and so are you!"

37

I calm down. Mam changes her clothes and puts on jeans and a jumper. She chats to a couple of her mates on the phone. She talks to somebody who's heard she's looking for staff. Mam says she is. She asks what qualifications and experience the person has. Is she interested in any particular aspects of salon work? Mam says she's building the business, and wants to build a proper team to help with it. She arranges for the person to come for an interview next week.

She puts the phone down.

"Sounds very nice," she says. "Young and bright and full of ideas. Mebbe a bit like me when I was as young as her."

"Like you still are, Mam," I say.

She grins.

"With the right folk, I'll make *The New You*

the finest salon in the north."

"You will, Mam. You're a star, Mam."

Koshka leaps onto her lap.

"And Koshka thinks you are too."

I stretch out on the sofa. I get *The Graveyard Book* and start reading. I guess I want everything to be ordinary for a while. I want an ordinary Saturday night with Mam, having some nice nosh, reading together, and watching some nice ordinary telly. She sits in her chair with Koshka on her lap. She's reading a book about the history of make-up. She says that thousands of years ago, in Greece and Rome, they used to paint make-up onto statues to make them seem real. She says that in some times and places, make-up was banned. They said it was a disguise, a fraud, a kind of lying. A sin.

She laughs.

"That'd be no good for me," she says. "No good for *The New You*."

After a while, we start cooking together. We're having cod and spuds and spinach. Great for the gut and the complexion, Mam says. We put everything into pots and into the oven. She sips some white wine; I swig some juice. We eat it at the table and she tells me about how, when she was a little girl, she got into trouble for painting her friend Nancy's face with watercolours and felt tips. Nancy's mam was furious. The green felt tip took a week to fade.

"Nancy didn't mind, though. She thought it was beautiful and so did I."

It starts to get dark outside. I eat a banana. Mam drinks some tea and says we'll watch some telly afterwards, shall we? I realize I've left the remote upstairs so I tell her I'm off to the loo. I go into the bedroom. The remote's on my bookshelf. I try not to even look at the wardrobe. I pick it up and turn back to the door.

Then I see it, the black van coming along the street with its headlights blazing. It slides to a halt behind Mam's van outside the house.

Marsh steps out.

Then Miss Crystal, carrying the black bag.

38

By the time I get downstairs, they're already at the front door. Mam's already opening it.

"Mr Marsh," she says. "Miss Crystal."

"Yes," says Marsh. "It's very nice to see you again."

Mam doesn't invite them in.

"Is Daniel at home?" says Marsh, but then he sees me over her shoulder. "Ah, yes, he is. Hello, Daniel." He puts that smile on his face.

"Hello, Mr Marsh," I say.

"It's very good to see you, lad."

Mam doesn't move.

"How can we help you?" she says.

"Oh, just a query, madam… I don't suppose we could step inside for a moment, could we?"

Mam glances at me. I want to tell her to send them away but I can't speak. She steps aside and in they come.

"It's about George," says Miss Crystal.

"I heard about him," says Mam. "What he was, what you did to him."

"Ah, he is our great achievement!" says Marsh. "I'll get to it quickly, as we have only a moment."

I clench my fists. My palms are sweating; my heart's thumping; I can hardly breathe. Miss Crystal stands by the hall table. Eden stays close to the door.

"You haven't seen George, have you, Daniel?" says Marsh.

I can see how cross Mam is. She doesn't like this bloke.

"Seen him?" she says. "Yes, he saw him, Mr Marsh, and he saw what you did to him."

Marsh shrugs.

"Yes, but have you seen him *since* then, Daniel?"

"How could he have seen George since then?" says Mam. "He's in bits. In his box."

Marsh ignores her.

"*Have* you, Daniel?" he says.

"How could I?" I force the words out. "He's gone. You took him away."

Marsh *must* see how nervous I am. He *must* be able to see that I'm lying.

"He's disappeared, Daniel."

"He's *what?*" says Mam.

"Disappeared. Probably taken by a rival corporation. But we must leave no stone unturned. Are you sure, Daniel?"

"No. I mean yes, I'm sure. That no, I haven't seen him."

He stares at me. I try to stare straight back at him.

"Mr Marsh?" says Mam.

"Yes?"

"Isn't it rather careless to lose a boy like George? To lose *any* boy?"

"He is not *any* boy. George One is a piece of revolutionary technology."

"That's not what I saw. I saw a boy, like any boy, who needed something nice to eat, who needed a bit of care and affection."

"Care and affection are irrelevant," says Marsh. "He is a product of years of research. He is entirely new."

"*All* children are entirely new," Mam says. "One day, long ago, even you and Miss Crystal were entirely new."

But I can see she wonders if Marsh was ever entirely new.

"No, madam," says Marsh. "You are wrong. This thing is different. It is a multimillion-pound investment."

"Well, you didn't take very good care of your investment, *did* you?"

Miss Crystal ignores her, turns to me.

"You know nothing?" she asks. "You've seen nothing?"

"Of course he's seen nothing," says Mam. "How

could he know anything about this? How dare you come into my house and talk to my lovely son like that!"

Miss Crystal reaches out as if to take Mam's arm but Mam wants none of it.

"We do realize that it is unlikely," says Miss Crystal. "And we're sorry to disturb you on a Saturday evening."

"But," says Marsh, "we do need to find him again."

"I think," says Mam, "that you've been with us long enough."

Marsh looks at me. He gives his smile.

"We'll find him, Daniel," he says. "We'll get him back where he belongs."

Out they go. Mam shoves the door shut behind them.

"Ugh!" she goes. "How dare they come and talk to us like that? I'm pleased they've lost him. They don't deserve him."

We go back into the living room. There's tears in Mam's eyes.

"Poor George," she says. "Poor lovely George. Whatever can have happened to him?"

"Dunno, Mam," I whisper.

She smiles and sighs.

"It's all a bit much, isn't it? Mates like George and a monster like Marsh?"

"Aye, Mam."

"How about watching something from way back in the past?"

"Eh?"

"Like we used to. *Postman Pat*, or *Rosie and Jim*?"

I laugh, but it's what we do. We put *Postman Pat* on. We watch programme after programme and we sit together on the sofa and we laugh and grin and sing along to the music and we know every single word and every single note and it's so great, like we've gone back to a time before any of this happened at all, like I've gone back to being a simple brand-new kid again.

39

I don't open the wardrobe that night. I want to forget about what's in there. It's all too much; it's all too quick. I put the pillow over my head. *Stop thinking,* I tell myself. *Stop remembering.* But I can't. I think about texting Maxie to tell him about Marsh coming over, but I don't want to do that either.

Stop thinking, I tell myself. *Just stop!*

And it must work at last, because next thing I know, I'm awake and the sun's shining and it's a new day. I get up and go down and have breakfast with Mam. There's church bells ringing somewhere and the birds are singing.

"Springtime Sundays," says Mam. "The best of all days."

"You say that about every day," I tell her.

"Do I?"

"You know you do. You say it about winter days as well, and about—"

"Ah, well. Maybe all days are the best of all days! What you up to today?"

"Dunno."

"Go see Maxie, eh? Have a wild time."

I shrug. Aye.

I text him. We arrange to meet at the cherry tree.

"What you going to do?" I ask her.

"Nowt. A blissful Sunday of doing absolutely nowt at all."

I don't look inside the wardrobe, but I check it's properly shut and off I go.

En route I have a few kicks in a little football match in Shelley Street. I buy some crisps at Wilf's Corner Shop. I start to get the lovely loose feeling of just being me, just moving through the place I know so well. I wave at mates, say hello to neighbours, growl at the fairy kids.

Maxie's waiting. He's eating a peanut butter sandwich. I give him some crisps and he shoves them in between the bread as well and he says that nothing more delicious has ever been known to humankind.

I tell him about Marsh and Miss Crystal, and I ask did they come to his house too.

"Nah. No reason. Why would they think I'm involved? Why would they think any of us are involved? They only tried you cos George came to your house for tea. They haven't got a clue, Dan. They think it's some other stupid robot company. Is George OK?"

I shrug.

"Aye," I say.

"Good."

He starts giggling and a bit of sandwich splutters from his mouth. He belches and lets out a massive fart.

244

"I had this dream!" he says. "I was a robot and me head fell off in assembly and Mrs Hoolihan said, 'Stop being such a silly boy, Maximilian!'"

I stuff crisps into my mouth and I giggle and splutter along with him.

"Aye," I say in a high voice, "stop being a silly, silly boy, Maximilian!"

"Nah! Why should I?"

"Because I'm telling you to."

"And who are you?"

"I'm the boss!"

"No, you're not!"

We lunge at each other and start wrestling, rolling about on the grass. We choke and laugh and splutter and tell each other we're silly, silly boys; and we go on fighting and laughing like that for ages till we're both knackered, and Maxie sits on my chest and says, "Had enough? Give up?"

"Aye," I say, and we roll apart and I say, "No," but we're too knackered to do anything about that. We just lie there under the tree, gasping for breath and feeling how sore our muscles are.

And we see there's an old lady with a shopping trolley standing looking at us.

"Are you two lads all right?"

"Yes," we say.

"And are you going to make up now and be nice to each other?"

"Aye," we say.

And she says that's lovely and off she goes again and me and Maxie laugh at the idea we have to make up and I tell him I hate him and he tells me he hates me.

We don't do much. We just wander about. We go to the swings park and swing on the swings. We poke a stick into a hole under a hedge where we know a stag beetle lives. It comes out for a minute, all black and shiny and looking like it's from Mars, then turns round and goes back in again. The stag beetle's like something from a nightmare. Years ago, we knew where another one lived. We used to be petrified when we made it come out like that. We used to run away screaming.

We wonder if we should call on Billy, but it's great being just the two of us. We pass Louise's house and we think about calling on her, but we hear her sawing away at the violin. Maxie says he's got to go back soon. They always have a Sunday supper with napkins and he has to wash his hair and put on a clean shirt for it.

"I've just got to put up with it," he says. "She'll give me dad some stick if I say I won't. And it keeps me on the straight and narrow, she says."

"That's what you need," I laugh.

"Aye, I know. Or I'll grow up to be a monster."

"You're one already, mate."

"I know. But she hasn't noticed yet. At least she's stopped expecting me to get born again. Mebbe next year, she said."

"That's good."

He laughs.

"Anyway, even if I did get born again I'd just want to be born again as me."

"So you'd still be Maxie Carr."

"Exactly! See you, mate."

"See you. Still coming for the George stuff tomorrow?"

"Course I am."

We look at each other, both thinking how weird that is, but we say nothing about it. We wander off in our different directions.

I'm happy. I always wanted a brother, and Maxie's like a brother as well as a mate.

I'm glad I've got my mam and not his dad's new woman.

Weird, how different families are.

When I go back past the swings, some fairies tell me to terrify them, so I do.

I tell them I know something that lives in a hole very close by that'd scare the living daylights out of them.

"Show us, show us!" they cry.

And I say no, they're too young; and they beg me to tell them, but I still don't and I know they're pleased that I don't.

Closer to home, Koshka comes and walks with me. I lean down and stroke him and murmur to him. I love Koshka. Couldn't imagine life without him. He's been with us since I was three.

Back at the house, I swing on the gate for a few moments, then in I go.

Mam's at the kitchen table with a mug of tea.

"Hiya!" I say.

"Hello, son. Can you tell me why George is in your wardrobe, please?"

40

There's no way to not tell Mam everything. So I tell her everything. She listens closely. She says she'd never have opened the wardrobe but she heard the cat scratching and scratching so went up to see what was going on. She thought Koshka must be after a mouse or something so she had to look inside.

"I nearly jumped out of me skin!" she says.

"Have you told anybody?"

She shakes her head.

"Who would I tell, Dan?"

"Dunno. The police or something."

"The *police?*"

"Aye. It's theft, or kidnapping, or ... I could go to jail for years and years."

"So that's a good reason *not* to tell them, isn't it?"

I'm crying now. Suddenly I can't stop.

We sit on the sofa while I calm down.

"I've been thinking while I've been waiting," she says.

"About what?"

"About how you've rescued him. About how proud I am of you."

"Are you?"

"Yes. I'm proud of all of you, Dan. It's kids like you that'll change the world."

"Will we?"

"And you'll protect it from the likes of Eden Marsh. Aye, he's very clever, and he can create amazing things, but he doesn't know how to look after those things. He doesn't know how to love them."

Then she giggles, like she's just a young lass.

"You've brought a robot into the house," she says. "Can I have a proper look at him?"

"Aye, Mam. You can."

41

Up we go. I shut the curtains then open the wardrobe door. Mam jumps with fright, but she takes a deep breath and settles down. He's just as we left him, standing there among the coats, dead straight and still with his arms by his side and his eyes closed.

Mam says he looks so lovely, so peaceful.

"Skin's nearly like yours or mine," she says.

She looks more closely.

"It's *like* our skin," she says. "Nearly human. But not really human. Too perfect."

"Too perfect?"

"Nothing's perfect, is it? Nothing *human*. You're not perfect, are you?"

"Hardly."

"But what would a man like Marsh understand about that?"

I get the multi-purpose remote from the shelf.

"What you doing with that?" she says.

I point it at him.

"You're joking!" says Mam.

I click. Nothing. I click again.
Still nothing. I click a few more times.

George opens his eyes at last.

"Hello, schoolmates," he says.

Mam claps her hand across her mouth and shifts away.

"It's all right, Mam," I whisper. "Are you OK, George?"

"I am perfectly splendid, thank you very much indeed," he answers.

I take his elbow and tug him gently and he takes a little step forward, then another. I guide him out of the wardrobe. The cat is at his feet.

"Kosh-ka," says George.

"Yes," I whisper. "Come on, George. Come into the room."

He steps further forward.

"Hello, George," Mam says in a trembling voice.

"George, this is Mam," I tell him.

"M-am," he says. "Mam."

"That's right. Come here. Sit down, mate."

I help him to turn, to sit down on the bed. He stares straight ahead, at the closed curtains. Koshka jumps up beside him. George rests his hand on Koshka's back and the cat purrs.

Mam sits down beside him. She feels his hair.

"It's real," she whispers.

"Is it?"

"Yes. Human hair. But so pale, like it's been bleached."

She contemplates it.

"We could change it," she says. "We could make it brown, or black, so that he blends in."

She contemplates him.

"I could change all of him," she says. "Give him the full makeover so he looks brand new."

"Mebbe," I say. "But it's not up to us. He's got to be like he wants to be."

"You're right," she answers.

"What would *you* like to be, George?" I say.

No answer.

"Do you want to be like us, George?"

No answer.

Koshka purrs.

Outside, it's already darkening.

Another day that's gone so fast.

253

"The others are coming tomorrow," I tell Mam.

"What will you do?"

"Practise a few things. Walking. Talking."

"Like when you were a bairn?"

"Aye. Like that."

I look at us, on the little rectangular bed in the little square room. Tomorrow there'll be five of us in here with the bed and the wardrobe and the shut curtains. It'll be so crowded. How can he practise being George in a room like this?

"We need to take him out," I say.

"Out?"

"I never like being stuck inside, do I? Why should George?"

"Would it be safe, though?"

"Cogan's Wood. You could drive us there in the van. Nobody'd see."

That's a better vision. Cogan's Wood, the place where I ran wild and free as a little kid, climbing the Witch Tree, splashing in streams, catching tadpoles in the lily ponds while Mam laughed and urged me on. I get a vision of George running wild like me, a kid of the estate, a kid of Cogan's Wood.

"There's still a few of your old clothes knocking about," says Mam. "He can wear those."

"What do you think, George?" I say to him. "Cogan's Wood tomorrow?"

"Co-gan's W-ood," he says.

"I showed you a drawing of it. Remember?"

No answer.

"It's magic," I say.

"Ma-gic."

I text the others. I tell them it's what we've got to do. He'll be able to walk and to run. He's been in a box and a van and a box and a wardrobe and a room. I say we want him to be free, don't we? And he'll start to be free, like us, out there in the woods. Mam'll take us there in her van and bring us all back home again.

They all say yes.

We'll take some food, some drink, some sweets. I'll charge him up tonight and bring the remote tomorrow.

Mam and I get George some old jeans and a green jumper. We put them on him. We put some old trainers on his feet.

"You're nearly like an ordinary lad, George," Mam says.

"We'll get him dirty," I say. "We'll get the dirt of Cogan's Wood on him."

She laughs.

"Aye. That'll be his makeover, eh? That'll make him new."

I practise walking with him, moving back and forth in my room. He steps forward. He swings his arms. He learns how to turn. Koshka walks and turns at his side.

"That's brilliant, George," I say.

"You're a natural, George," Mam says.

Then I think that maybe we've done enough for today. Maybe George can get worn out just like people do. And everything's so new and weird for him.

So I walk him towards the wardrobe and I open the door and try to guide him in.

He stops at the wardrobe door.

"It's just to keep you safe for the night," I say.

I push him gently but still he doesn't go in.

"N-no," he says softly. "No."

And suddenly I picture Eden Marsh pushing George into the black van. Maybe I'm being like Eden Marsh. Maybe there's an Eden Marsh inside us all.

So I guide George away from the wardrobe.

I sit him down on the bed and I sit beside him.

"I'm sorry, mate," I say.

I reach under the bed and pull out the blow-up mattress that's there, the one we use when Maxie comes for sleepovers. I blow into it until I'm nearly dizzy. Soon it's done. I lay it down beside my bed.

"This is where Maxie sleeps when he comes to stay," I explain.

"M-axie," says George.

I lie down on the mattress to show him what to

do. I take his hand and he lowers himself beside me.

He lies alongside me, looking up towards the ceiling.

Mam gets a pillow from my bed, raises his head and lowers it onto it.

She fetches a blanket from the wardrobe and lays it over him.

"That'll keep you warm and cosy."

I slide out from beside him. He turns his head and watches me stand up.

Koshka walks onto the blanket and lies down on him.

"We could read him a bedtime story," says Mam. "Maybe he'd like that."

"Aye, he would."

"Something gentle."

"*Postman Pat!*" I say.

She grins. Yes, that's the one.

I search my bookshelves. There they are, the *Postman Pat* books, all wrinkled and worn. How I loved them.

Mam reads a couple of the tales. I lie on the bed; George lies on the floor. Pat trundles with his cat Jess through the simple countryside. He trundles through my memories and my mind. I close my eyes and I'm a little boy again.

She finishes.

She sings the *Postman Pat* song. I hum along and soon George does too, in that squeaky groany way he did with Louise.

Then she stops singing and closes the book.

"And now it's time, my sleepyhead, to sleep," she says, just like she used to say to me.

"S-leep," says George.

"That's right, George," I say. "And then tomorrow it's Cogan's Wood."

"C-Cogan's Wood."

I get the multi-purpose remote.

"One day," I say, "maybe you'll learn to sleep like we do."

No answer.

Mam stoops down and kisses his head.

"Goodnight, George," she says. "Night-night."

I point the remote. I click. His eyes close.

We watch him lying there, dead still, on the blow-up mattress in my room. Then I twist off his ear with the five pence piece and I get the charger, plug it in and switch it on. Mam's jaw drops; her eyes widen. The low humming sound begins.

"So weird," Mam whispers.

She peeps through the curtains into the ordinary night, and then we go downstairs and have some sandwiches together.

Afterwards I have a shower and get into bed. I put the bedside light on and read *The Graveyard Book*. I keep looking down at him, at his hair shining in the light, at the cable pouring power into his head. I hear his humming.

When I sleep I dream that I'm little again. I'm

playing on the living room floor with plastic cars and vans. I'm trundling them across the carpet just like Pat's van trundles through the countryside. George is with me. He's small, too. He moves his cars. He shuffles around on the carpet with me, and I see that he's my brother; he's my twin.

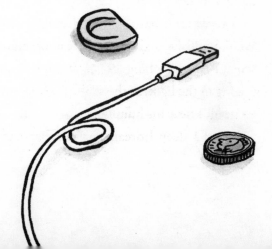

42

Next morning, there George is, lying exactly as he was the night before. I wake early and stare at him for ages, then I unclip the charger from his head. I twist his ear back on. I put some clothes on then get the multi-purpose remote.

I point and click.

Nothing.

I point and click again.

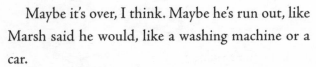

Nothing.

Again.

Nothing.

Maybe it's over, I think. Maybe he's run out, like Marsh said he would, like a washing machine or a car.

I try again. Again.

It all seems hopeless, then at last he opens his eyes.

"Good morning, schoolmates," he says in a frail and faraway voice.

I take his covers off.

"Good morning, George," I say.

He turns his eyes to me.

"Dan-iel," he says.

"Yes. Daniel."

I grin at him.

"I dreamed about you, George," I tell him. "Did you dream too?"

"Dream too," he answers.

Does he dream? What goes on inside his head when he's switched off? What goes on inside his head when he's switched *on*?

I stare into his eyes. Is there anything behind them except wires and connectors and switches and electronic chips?

I have to ask him, even though I know he can't reply.

"Do you think, George?" I say.

"Think George."

"Are you thinking now?"

"Now."

"You don't know what I'm talking about, do you?"

"Do you."

I tell him I'm dying for a pee. I go to the loo. I have a quick wash as well and then come back again. I tell him where I've been. I tell him about toilets and how everybody uses them. I say that peeing is the way I get rid of water from inside me, and the water comes from the food and drink I put in my mouth. I trace a line from my mouth down to my belly. I tell him that without water, I couldn't live. If I didn't have it, I would die. I think how weird that would seem to anybody that doesn't know about it.

George just looks back at me.

I wonder, Do you have to be a thing that can pee if you're going to be a thing that can think? Do you have to be a thing that can die if you're going to be a thing that can live?

"Do you pee, George?" I ask. I laugh out loud at the thought of it. He hasn't even got anything to pee with. I want to ask him everything but I know he'll have no answers.

"George," I say. "What's it like to be you, George?"

"You George."

Then Mam's voice is coming up the stairs.

"Come on, you two lazybones!" she calls. "The woods are calling."

George slowly lifts his head from the pillow and turns it towards the door.

"Dan-iel! Ge-orge!"

A little sound comes from his lips, like a fragment of a tune.

"M-Mam," he says.

"Come on, you lads!"

"M-Mam. Mam."

"Yes, George!" I tell him. "That's my mam. That's *our* mam."

I help him stand up. I guide him to the door. I tell him this is a door; these are stairs. I show him how to go down them, step by step, step by step.

Mam gives us both a quick hug.

"Good morning, sleepyheads," she says.

We sit down at the table.

There's toast. There's some fruit. There's tea.

I start to eat and drink.

There's a fragment of toast and a thin slice of apple and a tiny glass of water in front of George.

"These are for you, George," Mam says.

"They said he can only have…" I begin.

"I know that. But these are just tiny things. And

maybe he can have more than they think he can."

She lifts the glass of water to his mouth.

"Open wide," she says.

She touches his lips and they open. She gently tips his head back and trickles the water into his mouth.

"All gone," she whispers. "See?"

She helps him close his mouth again and shows the empty glass to him. She smiles and lifts the toast. She swings it through the air and makes an aeroplane noise as if it's flying, flying at last towards his mouth.

"Open wide," she says again.

He opens wide.

She flies it to his open mouth and pops it in. He closes his mouth. She laughs.

"Good boy," she says.

"Good boy," he says.

She does the same with the thin slice of apple. He eats it. Nothing happens.

"Was that nice?" I say.

"Nice," he answers.

"Mebbe," says Mam, "there's other parts of him that are human, just like his hair."

"Aye. Mebbe he's only half a robot."

"Mebbe he's even more amazing than they thought he was."

"Mebbe he'll turn into something they couldn't even dream of."

Mam holds his shoulders and looks into his eyes.

"George," she says, "you are a thing of wonder."

He blinks. He turns his eyes to me then back to Mam.

"Won-der," he says. "Won-der. Won…"

And then here's the others coming to the house and in through the door, and George names every one of them: Billy, Louise, Maxie.

They goggle at his clothes.

"That isn't our George!" says Billy.

"Oh aye, it is!" I say, and we all laugh.

Maxie and Billy have got little rucksacks with them. Louise has her violin case, like always. I grab my own sack. I put some sandwiches and the remote into it. Mam gets her boxes of bottles and brushes and scissors and creams and sprays.

Outside, the sun's shining bright. We check the street to make sure it's clear. It's still early; there's hardly anyone about. Mam takes her stuff and goes to the van and opens it. I walk George to the front door. I'm scared. What if someone sees? What if Marsh is watching? The open van seems a mile away.

"Are you ready?" I say to George.

"Rea-dy."

I take his elbow and guide him out. Maxie walks in front of us. I hear somebody calling my name. I look, and it's one of the Reception class fairies hand in hand with her mam. I wave at her. She leans to the side, watching us get to the van. She holds her hand up as a shade against the light. She shouts hello to Maxie and to Billy and Louise. They all wave back. Then she breaks free of her mam and comes running. By the time she gets here we're in the van, me and Maxie in the back with George in between, Billy and Louise in the front with Mam. Her eyes are wide with wonder.

"Hello, George!" she squeaks.

George turns his eyes to her. I lean across, trying to hide him from her sight. Mam turns on the engine.

"It's George!" says the fairy. "Isn't it? Hello, George! Remember me?"

I wind down the window. I shake my head and laugh.

"It isn't George," I tell her. "It's another boy named Alexander."

I laugh again.

"Aye, he probably looks a bit like George," I say, "but George is gone. They took George away last Friday."

She steps back. Her mouth droops.

"Did they?" she says.

"Yes. He's gone."

"Gone?"

"Yes. Gone."

The fairy's mam is with her now. She takes her hand again.

Mam laughs.

"Kids, eh?" she calls out to the fairy's mam, and we all sigh with relief as she drives us away.

43

We drive through the streets, past the pale houses, the little gardens, past kids playing out on the first Monday of the school holidays. We pass the cherry tree and our little branch library and Mam's *The New You* salon and Wilf's Corner Shop and the Green Man pub. Maxie passes a big bag of prawn cocktail crisps around. I take a little one and hold it out to George. He opens his mouth and eats. We all watch. Nothing happens.

When we were little, the woods seemed so far away, like they were in a different world, but now they seem so close. The estate comes to an end. There are a few old farm buildings left over from ancient times. There's a short narrow road then a bridge across a stream, and then the little iron gate and the path into the shadows and the trees beyond.

Mam drops us there. We all climb out.

"Look after each other," says Mam. "Have lots of fun."

"We will," we say.

"Bye-bye, George," she says as we guide him out.

"Bye-bye, Mam," he says.

She gets out, like she can't bear just to leave him. She straightens his jumper and puts her arms around him.

"Bye-bye, lovely lad," she says.

"Lovely lad," says George.

Then off she drives. And through the iron gate we go.

George walks just in front of me. He swings his legs in a regular rhythm. Each step he takes is exactly the same. He splodges through mud and puddles. His trainers get filthy; dirt splashes his jeans.

"That's right, George. That's great. Just keep on walking, mate."

"Walking mate," he answers.

Further, further in we go, through the shadows of the trees, along dry green paths and dark wet paths and through little dappled clearings. We pass the tumbled stones that used to be castles in ancient times, the black cross that marks the grave of the giant who will one day rise and walk again. We pass the place where wolves once howled, where fairies once danced, where pixies wait for passers-by to say the wrong word. We sidestep the hole in the earth that marks the entrance to hell, the place where brutal murder was done, where ghosts can be seen in particular light. We wander through the places where we've played and dreamed and terrified ourselves ever since we were little kids.

We move faster as we go deeper in. I feel my heart quickening, my breath deepening. George responds, and moves more quickly, too. A couple of times he stumbles and I reach out and help him find his footing again.

And we come at last to Witch Tree Clearing. The tree's at its centre, leafless and twisted and jagged against the sky. Once, this tree was a witch, till she was struck by lightning a hundred years ago and forged for ever into that shape.

"Away with you, Witchy Witch!" says Billy, as we used to do when we were young.

"Aye!" we all say. "Witchy Witch, away with you! We are not afraid of you!"

For a moment we forget about George and we

start running around the tree like we're little again. We flick the tree with our fingers; we kick it and thump it with our fists.

"Witchy Witch, away with you! We are not afraid of you!"

We're giggling and shouting, and we giggle and shout even more when George starts to copy us. He totters around the tree, punches it, kicks it, falls down, gets up again; and we love it and we urge him on. Then Louise gets her fiddle out and starts a spooky weird jagged tune that gets us dancing and whooping even more; and George tries to dance along with us, an awkward stumbling dance like the dance he did in school.

Then into the tree climbs Maxie, climbing higher than our heads.

"I've conquered the witch!" he yells. And then he screams, "Aargh, no! She got me!" And down he comes, jumping from the branches to the earth like he's been killed, but then he's up again and he goes to George and says to him, "She'll not get me, George!" And up he goes again while the rest of us dance and howl on the ground below.

Three times he does it, and three times he's killed; and on the third time he just lies there unmoving on the earth. We gather around him.

"Always happens, George," he exclaims. "Gets me on the third climb. And then, my dear friend… I'm dead." His eyes close and he lies dead still. His chest hardly moves at all.

"Poor Maxie," we whisper. "Poor dear old pal."

Now Louise plays slow, sad notes. We brush our cheeks, pretending to cry. George reaches out to touch his face.

"Maxie," he says softly. "Max-ie."

No response. For a long time, no response.

George continues to say Maxie's name.

Birds are singing in the tree above.

George looks up at them, and for a moment he starts to sing like them.

Then Maxie rises.

"I have come back!" he says.

He stands up and stretches. He walks around the tree, stiff-legged, swinging his arms stiffly. And George gets up and walks with him, and we all do, too, as we've always done.

And now it's Billy's turn to climb into the tree and then die, then Louise's, and then mine. And we all come back to life again and say we have come back. And we tell George that mebbe he isn't ready for tree-climbing yet, but he will be soon; and we do our wild running and screeching around the tree again and flop down and lean back against the terrifying trunk and say we're knacked; we're pooped.

And we all laugh out loud to see the dirt spattered across George's perfect face. He watches us laughing, then suddenly he topples to the earth and lies there, still as death.

We catch our breath. We lean over him.

"Oh no!" cries Louise.

But a moment later, he opens his eyes again.

"Have," he says in his soft sweet voice, "come back."

We all gasp and laugh with delight. And does George's face move, as if he is beginning to smile?

Almost, almost.

"Crisps!" says Maxie.

We all take a handful, and George reaches for one too, and we sit like that for an age, just being kids together, here in Cogan's Wood.

44

"What do you call a bloke with a spade in his head?" Billy says, just like he did when George arrived in our class.

We all groan.

"Doug!" says Billy. "Get it?"

We all groan again, but we laugh as well.

George just stares. How can he get it? How can we explain something like a joke to him? There's no way to even try.

"And what do you call a bloke without a spade in his head?" says Billy.

"Douglas!" we all snort.

"Here's one that fits," says Maxie. "Why did the monkey fall out of the tree?"

George just stares.

"Cos it was dead," says Maxie.

We laugh and groan.

"Doctor, doctor," says Louise. "I feel like a pair of curtains!"

"Pull yourself together, lass!" I say.

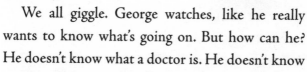

We all giggle. George watches, like he really wants to know what's going on. But how can he? He doesn't know what a doctor is. He doesn't know what curtains are.

I lean my shoulder against him.

"Don't worry, George," I say. He turns his eyes to me. "What do you call a deer with no eyes?"

"No idea!" the others yell.

"George," says Louise. He looks at her. "What's orange and sounds like a parrot?" He keeps looking. "A carrot!" she says.

He doesn't understand. He *can't* understand. But his face moves. His lips rise. We're all laughing. He shakes his shoulders. He makes a tiny laughing sound.

"Yes!" says Billy. "Yes! That's right!"

"What's brown and sticky?" I say.

"A stick!" we all yell.

"What time should you go to the dentist?" Maxie.

"Tooth hurty!"

We keep on laughing.

"Come on, George!" we yell.

He shakes, he squeaks, and we love him for it.

"What do you call a donkey with three legs?"

"A wonkey!"

"What did the rocket say to the moon?"

"Can't stop. I'm Russian!"

We go on. We tell more and more. We giggle and laugh. George shakes and squeaks. We laugh until we're all laughed out and our bellies are aching. We calm down. I put my arm around George.

"Maybe one day," I say, "you'll tell jokes to us. Do you think so, George?"

No answer.

And we all lean back against the Witch Tree and I say to George, "Are you happy, George?"

"Happy George," he answers.

And we all laugh at that, and we need say no more for a long time.

45

A bird flies low over our heads, softly screeching.

George turns his head to watch it pass.

"That's a bird, George," I say.

"Swallow," says Billy. "It's a swall-ow."

"Swall-ow," George replies.

Then I take George's hand and press it to the tree.

"And a tree," I say.

"Tree."

"Ash tree," says Billy.

"Ash-tree."

Billy crouches down and touches the ground. He guides George to crouch as well, to touch. He rubs George's fingers into the dirt.

"Earth," he says.

"Earth," says George. He looks at the earth on his fingers.

Maxie points past the tree into the emptiness above.

"Sky," he says.

"Sky," says George.

"Yes," says Louise. "Tree. Earth. Sky."

"Tree. Earth. Sky," says George. He looks at these things and seems to ponder them.

I gaze at the millions of things around us. Soil, grass, pebbles, leaves, crawling insects, flying insects, daffodils, clouds, fiddle, shoes, fingers, roots, dust, primroses, crisps, rucksacks, sandwiches. The million ordinary things that are all around us and that we all take for granted. But they're things that George will somehow have to get to know. Breath, light, shadows, all the sounds, all the hidden things as well as all the seen things, all the things that are far away as well as the things that are close. And as well as all the living things, there's all the dead things, too. Broken branches, dead trees. Bones of birds and animals lying in the dust, fallen leaves and fallen blossom turning back into the earth. Things dying so that new things can come to life.

How did he get to know so many things, like in class when he knew all the answers? How on earth

did *we* ever come to know so many things? Did somebody have to tell us everything and show us everything so we could make sense of it? And how come there's just so much? How come *the world* is here? How come *anything* is here?

Then Billy points to each of us: Maxie, Louise, Billy, me.

"People," he says.

He reaches out and takes George's hand and draws him towards us.

"People," he says again.

"Peo-ple."

"Friends," Billy says.

"F-riends."

"Family," I whisper.

"Fam-ily. Fam-ily."

And then, as if we can't help ourselves, we're off again, running this time away from Witch Tree Clearing towards the lily ponds.

46

Through more shadows and flashes of light we run, to the lily ponds. In summer the white and pink flowers bloom here and the leaves lie flat on the surface. Now in spring the leaves are spikes, rising from the depths below. We sit on the soft turf by the pools. The water's dark. We used to tell ourselves it went right down to Earth's core. We used to tell ourselves that monsters lurked down there. We used to see them, and we pointed them out to each other, and we dared each other not to run away screaming.

"Grass," we tell George. "Water."

We point to a sudden dragonfly flying low over the surface, the flash of little tadpoles, the gleam of big fish in the water's depths. He moves his eyes as we point.

"Dragonfly, George," says Billy. "Perch and carp. Minnows. Tadpoles."

"Tad-poles," he whispers.

We point into the sky to show more birds. We see a tiny mouse scuttling by the water's edge and we show him that. And insects in the grass, beetles on the water.

We laugh, as he seems to see them just as they disappear.

We tell him about the eggs and the brand-new chicks in the shrubs and trees around us. We tell him that this is spring, and we laugh again at the impossibility of getting him to understand.

We hear the bark of a distant dog, the rumbling of distant traffic, scuttlings in the undergrowth, the creak of a branch, the singing of birds. We can see the rooftops of the estate beyond the trees. Everything so far away, everything so close, everything so small, everything so huge.

We run out of breath trying to see and hear and name it all. And in the end we lie back on the grass and laugh at the impossibility of it. And George lies beside us, and makes a noise that sounds a bit like laughter.

And we open our rucksacks and get our lunch out.

"Food," says Billy, showing George a piece of cheese. Billy bites it, bites a piece of bread, swigs some juice.

George watches.

"Foo-ood," he says.

"That's right," says Louise.

She shows him a banana.

"Banana."

"Ba-na-na."

She snaps off a small piece.

"Would you like some, George?" she says.

"We shouldn't," I say.

"Yes," says George.

"Yes?" says Louise.

"Yes." And he takes the piece of banana and puts it in his mouth.

"More?" asks Louise.

She hands him more. He takes it, eats it.

"Ba-na-na," he says.

"Isn't it delicious?" says Louise.

"De-li-cious," he replies.

"Have this," I tell George.

I give him a piece of biscuit. He puts it in his mouth.

"Ba-nana," he says.

Louise passes him more banana. He puts it in his mouth. We all watch him. Nothing happens.

The sun gets warmer.

"We should stay here for ever," I say.

"Aye," says Maxie. "Live wild and free to the end of time."

"We'll eat berries and roots and leaves," says Louise.

"And rabbits and fish," says Billy.

"And who's gonna do the killing?" says Maxie.

"Me!" says Billy, taking out a little penknife. "You going to live out here, something's got to die." He shrugs.

"You going to live *anywhere*," he says, "something's got to die, even if it's just a banana."

We eat on, and think about that.

I bite into the biscuit. What had to die to help to make this?

"Sorry, banana," says Louise.

"Sorry, biscuit," I say.

We all snort with laughter, but it feels somehow right to say it.

"Thank you, banana."

"Thank you, biscuit."

We lie back and let the sun shine down on us. George lies between me and Maxie. He puts his hands behind his head like us. He sighs with pleasure like us. He stretches his hands into the air. He moves them before his eyes, follows them with his eyes. I reach up and touch his hand. He pauses but doesn't move his hand away. I look at our hands up there together, then I push my whole arm against his. I feel some resistance, then he pushes back. I laugh out loud and I roll on my side and grab him, like I do with Maxie when we have a fight.

Maxie's watching.

"Go on, George," he says. "Fight him back."

Billy laughs.

"Aye, gan on, George. Get him, mate!"

I laugh. How can he know what *get him* means? But I grab him again, by the elbow, and pull. He's more stiff than Maxie is; his arms and legs don't bend in the same way. I'm careful. I don't want to break him. But he seems so solid and strong.

"Fight back, George!" says Maxie.

I pull him harder. Then he suddenly puts his arms around me, like he wants to wrestle. I grunt and groan and he does too. I shove; he shoves. I pull; he pulls. Then I let him go and we both lie back on the grass. I sigh; he sighs.

"Good lad, George," says Billy.

"Good lad," says Louise.

Louise hums "All Things Bright and Beautiful", and we all hum along with her. George does his weird groany hum along with us. I want to yell out with joy, but I don't. It's like the singing birds are doing it for me, doing it for all of us.

Then suddenly George is up, and right at the pond side. He's crouching in the squelchy grass at the water's edge. He's staring down to where the fish and tadpoles are.

We watch him.

"He's OK," says Billy. "He won't fall in."

But we're ready to catch him if he does.

"Tad-poles," says George. "Fish. Water."

"That's right, George," says Maxie.

"See them?" says Billy.

George makes a noise like birdsong, high and sweet. He turns and looks at me. I shuffle closer until I'm right beside him, my head close to his. I look down. He gazes down too, and leans closer, closer to the water. There are the tadpoles, little black shimmering dots of new life.

He dips his fingers into the water, then his whole hand. He lifts up a little palmful of water with a few tadpoles flickering in it. He tilts his hand and back they fall. The surface of the water settles. He looks down into it, then at me, then back to the water again.

"Dan-iel," he says.

And then I see.

There are our faces, looking back up at us.

"Yes," I say softly. "That's me, George."

I take a deep breath.

"And that's you. George."

He dips his fingers in again. The reflections scatter and re-form. He dips again. They scatter and re-form. He leans down, until the tip of his nose touches the water's surface. He leans back again, and a pair of swallows swoop over him. He turns his head to follow them. He reaches his hands to them; he leans his head right back. They swoop again, again. He calls out to them and makes a birdlike squeak, a groan.

He doesn't look at us. There's just that strange singing. Hard to tell why, but it's all suddenly scary.

"Mebbe we should switch him off for a while," whispers Maxie.

"Aye," says Billy. "Mebbe it's all a bit too much for him."

"Mebbe we've overloaded him," says Louise.

"Mebbe we shouldn't have brought him at all," I say. "George?" I say. "George?"

And then he stands and he stretches his arms wide. He turns his face to the huge blue sky, to the birds, to the clouds, to the sun. He sways, he steps, he turns. He raises his arms as if they're wings. His song is suddenly clear and pure. It's truly like the song of a bird, a beautiful sweet noise that pours and pours from him. And he dances like a flying, swooping bird. He's smooth and elegant and wild. It's like the dance and song come from deep, deep down inside him, or as if they pour into him out of the sky and the earth and the water and the beasts and the birds.

And we sit on the earth to watch this boy made of metal, plastic, wires and switches and electronic chips and all kinds of technological wizardry, this wonderful boy who is suddenly free and wild and filled with crazy joy.

And we rise and join him.

And we dance and sing with George in Cogan's Wood.

Until he can dance no more, and he drops to the earth again. We all drop to the earth again.

And time goes by and doesn't seem to pass at all.

We don't know how long we lie there together in the brilliant light beside the lily ponds.

After a while, I touch George's shoulder. He looks straight back into my eyes.

"I..." he says.

"Yes, George?"

"I am..."

"I am what, George?"

47

George can't answer, and he's walking away, like something's pushing him.

Away from the lily ponds, away from us.

He's walking towards the narrow pathway that'll lead into the estate, towards the cherry tree. He doesn't look back. We get up and grab our stuff and follow him. Weird. On days like today there's often lots of kids around. Today there's nobody. There's kids' voices from the estate, kids' voices from other parts of the woods, but nobody near us.

George walks. The path's overgrown. The shrubs press in on either side; the undergrowth's dense and deep. It's been growing fast now the spring's here. He ploughs through it, struggles through it, twists his way through it. I catch up with him and the others tell me to hold him back. They say he'll be seen when we get back to the estate. He'll be taken away from us. But it's as if I'm scared of him. Or something like being scared. And I get the feeling that if I try to stop him it'll be worse. It feels like somehow I'm guiding him, even though I'm behind him.

Then we're through the tight pathway and we come to the edge of the woods, where the trees start giving way to fences and back gardens. And there's the brick houses and the pebble-dashed houses and soon there's the cherry tree on the beaten-down grass and the bench under the tree and the heavy pink blossom glowing in the afternoon light. And there are some kids, but they're moving away, kicking a football, and they don't look back. And cars pass by but none of them slow.

And George walks out from the path onto the green, and I pause and watch him. He gets to the tree and stands beside it and leans on it, and I see how he's wet from the pools and covered in dirt from Cogan's Wood; how he's like any kid who's come back from a messy day in the woods. And he turns to me like he's waiting for me, so I move on again and catch up with him, and he tilts his head to the side and looks at me like he's looking at me properly for the first time.

"I…" he says.

I say nothing.

"I am George," he says. "I am George."

48

And then the others arrive and we're all sitting under the cherry tree at the heart of our estate. We try to hide George by sitting around him but that just looks weird, so we act like there's nothing going on. A few kids pass by and see nothing strange so it seems to work. Louise realizes we need to tell my mam not to pick us up so she runs to *The New You* with the news. She comes back and says my mam was a bit worried about that but she was in the middle of a waxing session so there was nothing she could do.

The light's already starting to fade. I think we need to get George home so I tell him that.

We set off from the cherry tree, walking on the pale pavements by the black road between the pale houses. George is at my side, like any mate would be.

"Hell's teeth," says Maxie.

"What's up?" I say.

"Look," he says. Then, "Don't look."

We don't look, but we know the black van's here, gliding along a road that intersects with this one.

"Keep walking," Maxie whispers.

My heart beats faster. We walk. George walks with us. The van gets closer. It stops at the junction. Marsh and Crystal are in the front.

"Keep walking," Billy says in a low voice.

Marsh waves. I wave back.

We can hardy breathe. We want to run but we keep on walking. Dirty George walks at my side.

I wave again. Marsh gives a couple of quick toots on the horn, then he turns the corner and drives away.

And then we're at the gate and walking through the garden, then we're at the back door and we're in the kitchen.

And we punch the air and dance.

"They didn't realize!" says Maxie.

"They didn't see," says Louise.

"George," says Billy Dodds, "you're just like us."

And here's Koshka, coming through the cat flap; and there's George, bending down to welcome him home.

49

Billy makes tea. We all sit at the kitchen table. We eat bread and biscuits and cheese. George has the corner of a biscuit, a trickle of water. We talk about the games we played, the jokes we told. We talk about doing it all again another day.

"You enjoyed today, George?" asks Louise.

He looks back at her.

"Lou-ise," he says.

"Yes."

George is scruffy and tired after the long day, the same as we are. Koshka jumps onto his lap and George rests his hand on his fur. Koshka's tender body vibrates gently as he purrs, as his heart beats, as his breath flows gently in and out, in and out.

"Kosh-ka," murmurs George.

We go on eating. The day continues to darken outside. The lights in the windows of the estate

come on. Cars drift past in the roadway. Birds sing
their last brief songs. I switch our own light on and
I see a couple of Easter eggs on top of a cupboard
and lick my lips at the thought of them. I eat a
chocolate biscuit and sigh at the taste of it.

"Doctor, doctor," says Billy, "I feel like a bridge."

"What's come over you?" says Maxie.

"Three cars, two lorries and a bus," says Billy.

We all burst out laughing.

I can feel the day's air and sun on my skin.
There's dirt under my fingernails. If I close my eyes,

302

I see the Witch Tree, the lily ponds, the tadpoles, the narrow path to the cherry tree.

Mam must be working late tonight.

"What do you call a man with a seagull on his head?" says Louise.

"Cliff!"

"A woman with a pot of tea on her head?"

"Caff!"

"Br-own," says George.

We pause.

"Stick-y," he says.

"A stick!" we all yell.

Louise makes two fists. She laughs.

"You're learning so much, George!" she says.

We go on eating, drinking, chatting, sighing, joking.

After a while, Maxie looks at the clock.

"Have to be off soon," he says.

"Time to dress for dinner?" I say.

He nods and groans.

"What a life, eh?" he says.

"A life," says George, "is when a body exists and thrives."

We smile. That's right, we say. Oh, George, we say.

"A life is a growth and a decline," he says. "A life starts, continues, and then stops. It is the time between a beginning and an end."

He raises his eyes from Koshka and looks at us all.

"But life itself is endless," he says. "Life is the wonder of the universe. Life is the force that drives through time."

We're impressed.

"That's right," we say. "Well done, George!"

"I am George," he says.

"You are George," we agree.

Then Maxie has to go. He gets his stuff together.

"Been a great day, mate," he says to George.

"Mate," says George.

And Maxie goes, and the others get their stuff together and talk of leaving too.

George hangs his head; his shoulders droop. He looks so exhausted.

I say we should take him up and let him lie down and be charged up again. So up the stairs we lead him, step by step, me and Billy and Louise.

I pull out the mattress and down he lies.

We sit on the bed at his side. I plug the computer cable into the wall.

I've got the multi-purpose remote, but we can't bear to switch him off.

George starts humming the *Postman Pat* tune. We hum along with him. Koshka comes and lies on his stomach. I get Ted and put him on the pillow by George's head.

"Maybe he'll just go to sleep," says Louise.

"Aye," I say. "Mebbe."

Then they have to go.

"See you tomorrow, mate," says Billy.

"Night-night, George," says Louise, patting him on the leg.

"Tomorrow, mate." His voice is so soft and slow. "Night-night."

And then they're gone, and soon Mam comes home.

She's laughing about how much she has to do, about how many people want to come to her salon.

"It's cos you're brilliant, Mam!" I say.

"You!" she says.

She strokes George's cheek and softly laughs at him.

"Look at the state of you, lad," she says. "As bad as this lad of mine."

George gazes up at her.

"It all went well?" she asks me.

"Aye, Mam," I tell her. "Really well."

"You look sleepy, son," she says to George. "Time to close those bonny eyes."

"*Postman Pat, Postman Pat...*" she sings.

Softly, he hums along with her. Gently, she bends and kisses him.

"Happy, George?" she whispers.

"Happy George," he whispers back. Then he closes his eyes.

Carefully, I twist off his ear.

Carefully, I click in the cable and switch it on.

Then down we go, and I tell my mam about our day.

50

George doesn't wake up the next morning.

The power's been pouring into him all night. I get the remote and click and nothing happens. I click again and nothing happens. Again and nothing happens. Again and again.

"George," I whisper.

He lies there, dead still, just as he did last night. His eyes are closed.

I get dressed. I fetch Mam. She comes in.

"Oh, poor George," she says.

She goes to the bathroom and gets a bowl of warm water and a sponge. She washes the dirt from his face and hair. She cleans his hands. She brushes his hair.

"Maybe it's the cable, Daniel," she says.

But we both know it's not.

I click again and nothing happens.

"He had a lovely day, didn't he?" she says.

"Aye, Mam."

"And he had you lot."

She has to leave. She has to open the salon.

"Will you be OK?" she says.

"Aye, Mam."

I'm alone for a while with George and Koshka and Ted. I try the remote a couple more times, but I know there's no point.

Kids are playing outside. Birds are singing. There's traffic on the roads.

Billy arrives first, then Maxie, then Louise. I let them in and bring them upstairs.

Maxie runs home to get another cable. We try that. Nothing happens.

I take out the cable. I twist George's ear back on.

"They said he would come to an end," I say.

Billy's brought some spring flowers. They were for my mam, but he lays them on George's chest.

We shed a few tears together, but we all knew it would come to this.

Louise has brought her violin. She plays a sad and lovely tune.

Koshka lies down at George's side.

"How else could it end?" says Maxie.

Nobody says anything. For a few seconds, I have a vision of George walking the estate like us, going to school like us, growing older like us.

The vision fades.

"I am perfectly splendid, thank you very much indeed," says Billy.

"Good morning, schoolmates," I say.

"7693.7!" says Louise.

We giggle, despite it all.

Maxie's brought some crisps. He passes them round.

"You know what?" says Billy.

"What?" we say.

"He might be gone, but he had a day of proper life."

"Aye," we say.

"Better than being in bits in a box," says Maxie.

"Better than being in a museum," says Louise. "Better than being spare parts."

"Better than being with Crystal and Marsh."

We clench our fists and laugh.

"He lived!" says Billy. "We rescued George and he lived!"

And we stand up and do a little bit of our weird Cogan's Wood dance. Then we come back to ourselves and we know what we have to do.

51

We lift George onto my bed, and remember in silence the time we have spent with him.

Without anyone deciding it, each of us leans down and whispers softly in his ear. No one says what they have said to him.

Then we smile at one another and we know that the time has come. We do it so gently, so carefully. We take off his clothes. We remove his head, his arms, his legs. We disconnect the wires and switches.

We lay him tidily on my bed.

Just as before:

Billy will have the body.

Louise will have the arms.

Maxie will have the legs.

I will have the head.

Soon, George is carried away to different parts of the estate.

I put his head in my wardrobe. I'm left alone with Koshka as the day comes to an end.

I know that George will always be with me, that he will always be with each of us.

I know that *I* am George.

I know that every one of us is George.

I know that every morning when we wake, we are the new kids, born again.

We are the new kids, who will create a brand-new world.

THE BOY WHO SWAM WITH PIRANHAS

Stan's Uncle Ernie has developed an extraordinary fascination with canning fish, and life at 69 Fish Quay Lane has turned **barmy**! Then barmy becomes barbaric … and Stan runs away with the fair. Finally Stan has the chance to be the person he was meant to be. But does he have the courage to join the legendary Pancho Pirelli in the churning waters of the piranha tank?

"A life-affirming voyage of self-discovery with a fabulously fishy twist." THE BOOKSELLER

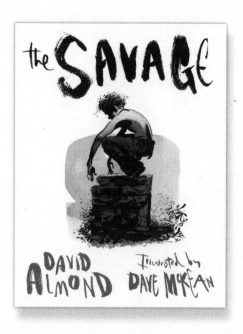

THE SAVAGE

You won't believe this but it's true.
I wrote a story called "The Savage" about a savage
kid that lived under the ruined chapel in Burgess
Woods – and the kid came to life in the real world.

*"An extremely touching and cleverly conceived
story within a story."* IRISH TIMES

THE TALE OF ANGELINO BROWN

Bert and Betty Brown have got themselves
a little angel. What a wonder! But not everyone
is happy about his arrival. Watch your back, Bert!
Watch your back, Betty! Evil is afoot...

*"Charming, funny and profound, exuberantly
illustrated by Smith."* THE BOOKSELLER

David Almond is the author of *Skellig*, *The Savage*, *The Tightrope Walkers*, *Bone Music*, *The Dam*, *The Boy Who Swam with Piranhas* and many other novels, stories, picture books, songs, opera librettos and plays. His work is translated into 40 languages and is widely adapted for stage and screen. His major awards include the Hans Christian Andersen Award, the Carnegie Medal, the Eleanor Farjeon Award, the Michael L. Printz Award (USA), Le Prix Sorcières (France) and the *Guardian* Children's Fiction Prize. He lives in Bath and Newcastle upon Tyne, the city of his birth. In 2021 he was awarded an OBE for Services to Literature.

Marta Altés loves to tell stories, and her passion for illustration saw her study for a degree in graphic design in Barcelona. She then moved to the UK to study for an MA in Children's Book Illustration at Cambridge School of Art, and she has since written and illustrated picture books such as *My Grandpa*, *I Am An Artist* and *NO!*, which won both the Read It Again! Award and the Nottingham Children's Award and was shortlisted for the Waterstones Children's Book Prize. Marta lives in London.